SO HAPPY TOGETHER

Emma sniffed in disdain. "Pity the countess didn't force *her* to ride with you. I daresay she has never ridden in a cabriolet before."

"Well, I will be happy to offer her the opportunity, you may be sure. No doubt it will afford me more pleasure than the termagant who rides with me presently," Adam declared, thoroughly fed up with the beautiful Miss Lawrence at the moment.

"How dare you speak so to me! Why, of all the nerve!"

"My dear Miss Lawrence, you would be amazed at the things I dare to do. May I suggest you take a more conciliatory path? Otherwise, I might be tempted to do what your governess so obviously failed to accomplish."

Adam turned to her and grinned wryly.

"I am told paddling is most salutary. . . ."

"When Ms. Hendrickson's name is on the cover, you know you'll be satisfied when you turn the last page."—Jane Bower from *Romance Reviews Today*

THE MADCAP HEIRESS

Emily Hendrickson

A SIGNET BOOK

SIGNET
Published by New American Library, a division of
Penguin Group (USA) Inc., 375 Hudson Street,
New York, New York 10014, U.S.A.
Penguin Books Ltd, 80 Strand,
London WC2R 0RL, England
Penguin Books Australia Ltd, 250 Camberwell Road,
Camberwell, Victoria 3124, Australia
Penguin Books Canada Ltd, 10 Alcorn Avenue,
Toronto, Ontario, Canada M4V 3B2
Penguin Books (NZ), cnr Airborne and Rosedale Roads,
Albany, Auckland 1310, New Zealand

Penguin Books Ltd, Registered Offices:
80 Strand, London WC2R 0RL, England

First published by Signet, an imprint of New American Library,
a division of Penguin Group (USA) Inc.

First Printing, September 2004
10 9 8 7 6 5 4 3 2 1

Printed in the United States of America

PUBLISHER'S NOTE
This is a work of fiction. Names, characters, places, and incidents either are the product of the author's imagination or are used fictitiously, and any resemblance to actual persons, living or dead, business establishments, events, or locales is entirely coincidental.

Chapter One

"There's no point in lingering here." Adam Herbert turned from the window to face his father. "I could wait for years and years before I obtain a curacy. There are no vacancies to be found anywhere. And even where the minister is as old as Methuselah or often absent, it is impossible to get rid of a clergyman once installed. He can be dreadful!"

He thrust his hands in his pockets, wondering what his father would say. It wasn't that Adam truly wanted a parish. His father expected now that he had finished Cambridge he would begin his calling—if he indeed had such.

With a deep sigh, Mr. Herbert nodded a reluctant agreement to the undoubtedly factual conclusion, since he refused to ask favors. "What do you intend to do? You might consider law." This was a hesitant suggestion, diffidently made.

Adam turned slightly to stare out of the window again. How could he tell his father that more than anything he wanted to manage some land, to know the satisfaction of growing things? He had not opposed his father's assumption that he would follow in his footsteps. The problem was that those footsteps were ably occupied, and there was no sign of opportunity for a young, not-too-eager man for a decent position even as a curate—and the thought of living on eighty pounds per annum wasn't exactly appealing. If he were fortunate to obtain a vicarage, he might garner one hundred and fifty to begin. If he was lucky.

"What I would like to do," he mused aloud, "is travel a bit." Taking note of his father's alarmed expression, he added, "Oh, not out of the country into foreign parts. I would like to see where your family lives, where you grew up and spent your boyhood." He waited for a reaction.

Mr. Herbert gave Adam an amazed look. "You have never expressed any wish to do something like this. I thought you cared nothing for the family tree or relatives."

"Well, perhaps not the tree, but I am intrigued by your uncle, the Earl of Stanwell. Priscilla mentioned meeting his grandson in London." He gave his father a hopeful look, for this elusive earl piqued his interest.

"Aye. Your sister said the viscount is a dandy of the first water." Mr. Herbert grimaced. "Although, she did say he had excellent manners and is accepted everywhere."

"However that might be, I should like to meet the earl, if possible. Even if I don't, it would be nice to see the estate, the village where you grew up. You approve?" he concluded as he observed a smile slowly crease his father's face.

"I think it a splendid notion." The rector thought a moment before continuing. "But if you intend to travel you will need your own vehicle. There is no point in trying to take a stage only to be afoot when you get there. It just so happens Lord Latham mentioned he wants to sell his cabriolet. It looks good to me and will only require one horse. We will find you a sound animal and you can be headed west before you know it."

Adam grinned. "I almost have the feeling you will be glad to see me gone!" He felt well nigh light-headed with relief that his suggestion was so well received.

"Never, you must know that. But a restless lad can too easily find trouble when not gainfully occupied. Go with my blessing. Who knows, perhaps you *will* meet my uncle. Stranger things have happened. The earl is considered to be a remote gentleman, more so since his son William died."

It seemed as though the trip was meant to be, for the cabriolet was in Adam's hands before another day was out, and the squire sold him a horse at what Adam suspected was a very low price. He thought the chestnut named Jigg looked rather fine pulling the shiny black cabriolet. He took a day to pick out the wheels with a bright yellow paint, liking the touch of color on the smart vehicle. He polished the glass-and-wood folding screen that added protection from the weather. The damaged leather apron was soon mended.

Adam's clothing was a sore point with his mother. She saw to it that his garments were washed and pressed, all the while complaining at the paucity of his wardrobe. His sister Tabitha brought him several new neckcloths. But fine Marcella waistcoats and coats of the best Bath cloth were beyond his purse. Still, he looked acceptable, his auburn hair neatly styled. He was taller than his father, but his gray eyes had the same keen look of intelligence in them.

He stowed his portmanteau behind the cabriolet seat on the small platform where a groom might be if he had one. His luggage was as modest as his clothes. He turned back to pat his mother on her shoulder. "I don't mind, you know. I have never been one to long for fine feathers."

"It was just in case you met your great-uncle. I'd not

have him think your father a failure because he sees us as shabby-genteel sort of folk. First impressions can be lasting ones." She gave him a bright smile with a hint of tears.

"I'd soon set him straight on that." Enduring the hugs and handshaking with goodwill, Adam eagerly set forth west. Somehow he would manage to see the earl—one way or another. The letter of introduction handed him by his father might be the thing.

Not in any hurry, he took his time traveling, enjoying the sights to be found on his route, bent on taking care of Jigg. It was two weeks later that he slowly entered the picturesque village of Peetbridge, on the edge of his great-uncle's estate.

The sun warmed the honey-colored stone of neat cottages that lined the main road. Flowers bloomed beneath white-painted window frames where curious occupants peeped out to see who this stranger might be. It was much like home. He studied the various shops as he drove along the main street of the prosperous village. They were a handsome collection, with stone fronts and bowed windows to display the wares.

The Feathers, the village inn, appeared to be a successful concern. It had the look of a snug, comfortable place. He wheeled his cabriolet through the attached arch into the yard. An ostler hurried forth to take the horse and carriage, leaving Adam to take his portmanteau and venture through the large oak door. Once inside, he was impressed with the neatness and cleanliness of the place. Since he had progressed slowly so as to spare his horse, he had stayed in a fair number of inns. This was clearly superior.

"Good day to you, young gentleman." The innkeeper

appeared from a back room, bustling to greet his new guest.

Adam felt he was being assessed. "I should like a room for an indefinite period. My father came from around here and I've a notion to see the country, perhaps look up relatives." He gave the man a straight look in the eye.

The innkeeper thrust the visitor's book toward Adam, then looked at his signature when he'd signed. "Herbert?" He studied his guest again. "Aye, you've the look of them—with that rusty hair and gray eyes. Whyn't you at Stanwell Hall? The earl's in residence."

"I've never met the man. Something I hope to rectify. I could scarce impose, not knowing my great-uncle."

The innkeeper nodded, then told a maid to usher Adam to his room. It seemed clean, with a fine-looking bed and a window with a view of the street below.

Adam disposed of his things in the wardrobe and chest, then tidied his clothes. A hasty glance at the looking glass showed his hair acceptable. The gray eyes gazing back at him revealed his inner excitement. At last he was really here. He set his hat on just so, and then hurried back down, wishing to see as much of the village as he could before dark.

At the foot of the stairs, the innkeeper caught his eye. He gestured to a man seated in the common room. "That be his lordship's steward there, just come in. Name of Chambers. Might introduce yourself." The innkeeper nodded to a lean gentleman of middle height and years wearing a brown coat and tan breeches. He was enjoying a mug of ale along with some bread and cheese.

Adam did just that at once, introducing himself with a modest bow. He pulled out a chair when motioned to sit down.

"A Herbert? You would be Robert's grandson, then? George's son, I reckon." Clearly knowledgeable of the family tree, the steward studied Adam, waiting for confirmation.

"My father is George Herbert. He is the rector at Rushcombe, Kent. One of my sisters has resided with our Aunt Mercy in London, where she met Viscount Rawlinson. Her talk of relatives prompted me to see where my father grew up, the countryside and all. And . . . perhaps meet my great-uncle as well." Adam figured he might as well put his cards on the table immediately. This was not a moment to be shy and retiring.

Mr. Chambers asked a number of penetrating questions, in particular about Adam's plans for the future.

"Not having any secure post, I am at loose ends at the moment. I shall come about, I'm sure." Adam gave the man a forthright smile. He had no intention of pretending to be other than he was.

"Interesting. I shall mention your being here to his lordship later when I return." Mr. Chambers clearly was not a chatty chap, seeming quite reserved.

"If there is a possibility that I might see the estate, I should enjoy that very much," Adam added. "Even if I don't meet my great-uncle, I should like to see the house and land."

The steward nodded, but no reply was forthcoming.

Adam thanked the man, then excused himself on the pretext of seeing the village. He had no desire to intrude on the man's privacy. He probably had little time to himself if his life was anything like that of the steward at Latham Court.

The village of Peetbridge dozed peacefully in the midday sun. Adam sauntered along the well-swept pavement, pausing to admire the contents of the pastry shop window. The peace of the village was shattered when he heard an argument not far off. A woman was strongly protesting something. Not liking the sound of it, he headed that way. His steps brought him to a small herb garden beside the pastry shop, where a young lady fended off the advances of a chap Adam remembered from Cambridge.

"Polkinghorne! What a surprise to see you here!" Adam entered the garden, his long legs covering the ground in seconds. Claude Polkinghorne had been a fellow who liked to pick on the weak, those who could ill defend themselves against his strength. Adam hadn't liked him then, and liked him even less when he observed the beauty he intimidated.

"Herbert! What the devil are *you* doing here?" The bully took a step from the young woman, giving Adam a cold, condescending stare designed to send him away.

Adam smiled and bowed to the woman who eyed him with patent misgivings. She was the prettiest girl he could recall seeing anywhere ever, with dark blue eyes and a sweet mouth in a classically oval face. Soft brown hair framed her face in a very fetching manner. A few curls teased his eyes where they escaped from her bonnet, a fine affair of chip straw and ribbons.

Ignoring Claude, he gazed into her eyes and announced, "I am Adam Herbert, as Polkinghorne would tell you if he had his wits about him." Glancing at Claude, then back to the unknown beauty, he continued. "I thought to visit this area to discover something of the place where my father grew up."

"You are related to the Earl of Stanwell," she declared. Seeing his faint surprise, she added, "You have the Herbert looks—the auburn hair, gray eyes, and the nose. Not that your nose is anything remarkable, but it is a nose you see again and again in the family." She attempted to shake off Claude's hold and failed.

Claude snickered.

"Well, I am not ashamed of having a family nose. Besides, from all I have heard, the earl is a very esteemed gentleman. Unlike some others." The look he sent Claude was meant to remind him that Adam was privy to any number of unsavory incidents in Claude's Cambridge days. But Claude stood firm, unwilling to yield an inch. Only after Adam took a step in his direction did Claude release his hold on the young lady's arm.

The beauty took several steps away from Claude to stand by Adam, something that pleased him mightily.

"Claude is my cousin," she said, glaring at the affronted gentleman. "And you truly had no need to come to my aid, although I suppose I must thank you anyway. I am quite able to handle the nitwit. I have been doing so for years." Her sniff was clearly one of disdain.

Adam didn't know what to think of her outspoken manner. He had to admit that Claude would cut a fashionable swath in any village with his well-cut coat of peacock green over tan breeches and a bronze waistcoat. His boots had a blinding shine, reminding Adam that he needed to polish his before tomorrow. Claude's hat was of the finest beaver and tilted at a rakish angle over his brow. But Adam also knew the sort of fellow he was under all that polish.

"Since my dear cousin has lost his manners, permit me to say that I am Miss Lawrence of Brook Court." She dipped a proper curtsy. It wasn't all that often that a handsome gentleman visited Peetbridge or the area, for that matter. The chaps who came to see her cousin were a dreadful sort, dandies all of them. Or worse. She had no use for any of them, but particularly cousin Claude.

Claude sputtered. "Dash it all, Emma, 'taint proper for you to introduce yourself."

Emma flicked him a look that should have felled him on the spot. "Well, perhaps in the future you might learn some conduct, Claude." If he thought that she would yield to his crude notions of a courtship he was far and away off. She would as soon be a spinster the rest of her life!

"Might I escort you to wherever your destination might be?" Mr. Herbert asked with a bit of reserve, as though not sure what she might say to him. Emma liked his reticence, something her stupid cousin had never learned.

"I was bound for the pastry shop when Claude tried to . . . what were you trying to do, Cousin?" She firmed her lips and tapped a daintily shod foot.

"Dash it all, Emma, I seldom get a chance to talk to you." His mouth turned down in a sulky pout, as petulant as a thwarted boy who has had his toy taken from him.

"You have nothing to say that *I* wish to hear." She narrowed her eyes. "Simply leave me alone, Cousin."

Sensing there was a great deal more to this scene than he was being told, Adam offered his arm without comment. She accepted with amusing reluctance. He liked the sensation, though, feeling like a regular knight-errant.

"Now see here, Herbert." Claude took a threatening step forward. "No need to interfere with that madcap."

"I believe I will, however." Adam bestowed a triumphant smile on a man he cordially detested. He then escorted Miss Lawrence from the miniscule garden to the door of the pastry shop, ushering her safely inside.

"My thanks to you, Mr. Herbert." She curtsied again, offering a polite smile. "Although, I repeat that I could have managed my cousin without your intervention." Her chin tilted up in what appeared to be defiance. Adam was tempted to tell her what Polkinghorne had done while at Cambridge, only it wouldn't be fit for her tender ears.

She was dismissing him, and he was reluctant to leave her with Polkinghorne lingering about outside. Yet, if she persisted in being so dratted uppity, perhaps she merited her cousin's attentions.

"You will be safe?" Adam queried, although why he should be concerned with this impudent piece eluded him.

"A maid is with me. Claude had told her to go away." She gave a small woman garbed in gray a narrow look. "I will not have her accompany me again. Claude has a way of intimidating the servants. They seem to think I will succumb to his blandishments and marry the clod."

"You do not hold your cousin in high regard, I gather." Adam waited while she selected an assortment of pastries, then walked at her side when she left the fragrant warmth of the little shop.

Once outside and away from the inquiring eyes and ears of the baker's wife, she answered him. "No. He was an utter toad as a child and age has not improved him. I have the feeling that you know him fairly well." She turned to gaze at him with patent curiosity.

Adam glanced off to see Polkinghorne in the distance, not far from The Feathers inn. "True. We were at Cambridge at the same time."

She grimaced. "How fortunate for you. I suspect you could offer some famous tales of his exploits." Her voice held a dry note. She walked a few steps to where a gig awaited her, the groom watching Adam with suspicious eyes. "You intend to meet the earl?"

"I would like to. I have heard such interesting stories about him. He is my great-uncle, and from what my father has said, that house is just as fascinating as he is."

"If you like collections and old things and the like, it is. You plan to remain here for a time?" She paused by the carriage, turning to face him.

Adam repressed a grin at her forwardness. It wasn't the done thing for a young lady to be so curious about a stranger. She was indeed a madcap. If staying in Peetbridge meant he might see her again, he would stay as long as possible. "Yes. Even if my great-uncle is not interested in meeting me, I should like to explore the area."

She entered the gig and with capable hands took the reins from the groom. "I would not be the least surprised if he summons you to Stanwell Hall. He is not given to much entertaining, but he is a curious man. You wait and see. You will have the opportunity to go through the entire place."

The maid went around to the far side and climbed into the gig, waiting with sullen patience.

Adam tipped his nicely brushed beaver hat. "I shall look forward to seeing you again, Miss Lawrence. Perhaps you can instruct me on the history of this area?"

"There is a decent guide book available. The Feathers ought to have a copy." Her gaze swept over him, reminding Adam that he had been a bit too forward with a young woman he didn't know, never mind that she had done the same.

Adam stepped back, acknowledging her curt, but admittedly proper, set down. He earned it. No matter how much he would like to spend time with this beautiful creature, he was a stranger about whom she knew nothing, other than that he was a member of the Herbert family. He watched as she deftly flicked the reins, departing without so much as a glance in his direction. Miss Lawrence did not flirt.

Emma capably guided the gig from the village back to her home. Brook Court might not be as splendid a place as Stanwell Hall, but the manor house was old and supposedly had entertained some famous people at one time or another.

While they clipped along at a smart pace she considered what had happened in the village. Really, she must persuade her father to convince Cousin Claude to leave her alone. Unless dearest Papa had succumbed to the notion that Claude would make an acceptable husband for her. Horrors!

This thought was so dire that she nearly dropped the reins. Only the dismayed gasp of the maid brought her to her senses.

Once at Brook Court, she left the gig in the care of the groom and ignored the subdued maid as she went to seek out her father. She found him in his study, a paneled room with ample space for his desk and books.

"Papa, I have returned from the village with your special pastries." She placed the neat parcel on his desk. "Tell me, what do you think of my cousin Polkinghorne?"

"He's not a bad sort of chap." He frowned at his only child from beneath bushy gray brows. "Have you had a run-in with him again?"

" I want you to know that no matter what, I will not marry Claude Polkinghorne. He is an utter toad!"

"Looks well enough to me."

"I met someone this afternoon who knew him while at Cambridge. He did not appear to have a high opinion of my cousin."

Mr. Lawrence leaned back in his chair, one finger

marking his place in the book he had been reading. "A stranger here? Who?"

"George Herbert's son, Adam. He rescued me from Claude."

"He did, eh? Well, we shall see about that."

"What do you mean by that, Papa?"

"Er, nothing," he said, his gaze sliding away evasively. "You know the earl. Mr. Herbert will be called there in a trice."

Emma was pleased at the thought. Any man who could put Claude Polkinghorne out of countenance was one she could admire!

Chapter Two

"It is as Mr. Chambers told you. Mr. Adam Herbert, your great-nephew, is staying at The Feathers in the village." Emma gave her old friend and neighbor an impish look. "I believe he would like to meet you. Are you curious about him?"

The Earl of Stanwell leaned against his high-backed armchair to study her where she perched on a nearby chair. "You believe him when he claims to be a Herbert?" He rubbed his chin, intrigued with the news she and Mr. Chambers had brought to him.

"Definitely. Not only does he have a well-bred air about him, he also has that lovely auburn hair and gray eyes, *and* he has the Herbert nose." She suspected her voice had a touch of mischief in it, and probably her eyes as well. Emma knew that the particular combination of hair and eye color combined with the claim to the Herbert nose would arouse the earl's curiosity.

"The Herbert nose, my dear? And, pray tell, what is so particular about *my* nose?" the earl growled.

She wasn't fooled in the least by his show of fierceness. She had long suspected that underneath that stern exterior existed a sentimental heart.

"It really exists, you know. If you study the paintings in the gallery and halls around this vast pile, you will discover what you probably know and may not admit—you all have the same nose. Come to think on it, auburn hair and gray eyes stay in the family as well." Emma tilted her head, casting a glance at the earl, then to a painting that hung over the mantel of the great hall fireplace. "Look. You can see it in the painting of your father."

The earl did as bid. "Well," he muttered, "one painting does not account for them all. I suppose you think I ought to invite this young scamp to stay here?"

"Well, he came to my rescue like a knight-errant when Claude was being tiresome again, so I don't think he's a scamp. Those long legs of his reached us in seconds." She thought for a few moments, considering the matter. "I don't think Claude likes him, and I am quite certain Mr. Herbert does *not* like Claude. He looked at him quite as though my vexing cousin was a nasty sort of insect recently crawled out from under a rock. It was delightful the way he intimidated Claude into releasing my arm." She shrugged and chuckled at the memory. "I must say, he cowed Claude rather quickly. I can't help but wonder what Mr. Herbert knows about Claude."

"Why does your father allow that puppy to bother you?" the earl demanded. Then he thought a minute before continuing. "But, now you have me intrigued. Anyone who can see through your cousin is bound to be agreeable. So, shall I send a footman to fetch young Mr. Adam Herbert here?"

"Indeed, do. But do not send your coach. I believe he has his own carriage, for the pastry shopkeeper told my maid that the newcomer owned a superior vehicle and a fine horse. One of your suitably imposing footmen ought to impress the village to a man . . . and woman."

"Oh, ho! Is the young man more than presentable?" The earl's gaze pierced Emma's calm mien.

Emma was glad that she didn't blush easily. Even her

old friend could discompose her at times. "Aye, I should say he would please you. He is no blot on the family tree at any rate. At least from what I could tell." And that was an understatement if she had ever made one. "Mr. Herbert is a gentleman of handsome appearance."

His gray eyes had flashed with anger when he found Claude using her so ill. She had been only too glad to take refuge beside that tall, well-built man. Claude wouldn't actually harm her, but he could be so annoying.

"I would say he would be an addition to any gathering and likely have many young ladies swooning over him," Emma added. When Mr. Herbert had parted from her side, the memory of his engaging smile had lingered in her mind for quite some time. She had tried to be severe, not wishing to give him the impression she was a hoyden. But she'd not be averse to having that smile trained on her again.

The earl rubbed his chin for a few moments, then summoned his butler, a fellow who was a contemporary of the earl, only more white on top, something that pleased the earl no end. After giving Newton instructions regarding young Mr. Herbert, the earl returned his attention to Emma.

"So, what shall I do to entertain this fellow? For I am certain you have something in mind." He rubbed his chin again, looking to Emma for her reaction.

"No assemblies are to be had in the summer, I fear. This is true for any theater or musical presentations as well, not that we ever go. Perhaps you might offer a musical evening or a ball here? You have not given a ball in ever so long, and I do love to dance." Emma hoped this might be the case. Since her mother died there had been little or no entertaining at Brook Court and a trip to Salisbury for an assembly simply didn't happen.

"Have I mentioned recently that you are an impertinent miss?" He waggled a finger at her in admonition. "Yes, I know you love these affairs."

"Especially since Papa cannot or will not do anything. How I am to find a husband when he will not give me a Season in London much less attend an assembly in Salisbury or stay in Bath is beyond me." This particular neglect especially irked her. As much as she loved her father, she wanted to marry and have a family of her own. The thought of lingering on at Brook Court into spinsterhood was enough to give her the green melancholy.

"You think young Herbert might do?"

"No! I did not say that. Actually. It is just . . . I long for some gaiety, music, and laughter. Our house is become dull and dreary. Don't you know that is why I am here so often?" She flashed him a wide and totally unrepentant grin.

"Ha! I knew it wasn't the pleasure of my old company. Summon the tea tray and I will consider what you have said. I shall consult with Sophia about it."

Emma compressed a smile. "I suspect the countess will agree with me. I believe she enjoys planning parties as much as I enjoy attending them."

"Conspiracy! That's what it is. You women." The earl frowned, looking fierce.

"And what is the matter with us women, pray tell?" the countess cried, entering the room in time to hear the earl's last remark.

Emma rose to curtsy to the charming older lady, who was always dressed in the latest style from London. "Your husband was contemplating what we might do to entertain his great-nephew when he comes."

"I was unaware we were to have company. Charles, did you mention it and I forgot?" She approached her husband, giving him a shrewd look.

"Emma just informed me that a young Mr. Herbert is in the village at The Feathers. George's son, I should imagine. Come here to see the area and if possible this pile of old stones."

"And to meet you as well, my lord," Emma reminded.

"Hmpf." The earl glared at her again.

"I recall meeting your nephew George many years ago," Sophia said. "He seemed an amiable gentleman. I believe he had five daughters in addition to this son?" The countess seated herself in a matching high-back armchair, placing her feet neatly upon a small stool, for she was much shorter than her husband, as well as younger.

"If you know, why ask me?" the earl snapped out in his customary testy manner.

The countess turned to Emma, pinning her in place with a questioning look. "What does this young man look like, pray tell? I assume you met him?"

"Indeed. He rescued me from Claude. Mr. Adam Herbert is quite tall and slender, although of athletic build, with auburn hair and fine gray eyes. He beats old Claude to flinders as looks go."

"She says he has the Herbert nose. Is there a Herbert nose, my dear?" the earl demanded, sending his wife a challenging look.

"Of course there is, Charles. Emma has the right of it. It will be interesting to see this young man. You sent for him, of course?" She raised her brows in question.

"Hmpf."

"Which means of course he did," Emma said with a smile.

"Folderol. Need to entertain him, I suppose?" the earl grumbled.

"Indeed, but nothing very taxing," the countess agreed. "I should imagine he would like to see a race or two and we can give a ball here. Nothing much going on in Salisbury or Marlborough in late summer," she concluded.

"The *Journal* lists few activities to be had," Emma replied, trying to recall what she had found in the *Salisbury and Winchester Journal*. "Fellows' Library received a new shipment of books. I sent off a request for several of the latest novels," she added quietly, knowing what the earl thought of novels.

"I should think you might have learned to appreciate something more than novel reading at that expensive boarding school your father placed you in all those years."

"Mrs. Cambell saw to it that I had the finest of music lessons, sirrah! There is no better teacher to be found in all of Salisbury," Emma retorted, darting a glance across the room where the fine harp stood. How she adored her harp. The ethereal music that floated forth soothed her heart, comforting her.

The earl nodded in the same direction, where the exquisite harp sat next to a long window that offered splendid light for seeing the music placed on the polished stand next to it.

"I gather you wish me to play for you?"

His dark gray eyes met hers. "One of the reasons I tolerate your impertinence, my child, is to be entertained from time to time with the harp. I calculate it will help me appreciate the music when I get to heaven."

"Oh, pooh," Emma exclaimed. She jumped up from her chair to drop a light kiss on his elderly head before she made her way to the beautiful instrument.

Emma intended to be part of the music festival in Salisbury come next St. Cecilia's Day. Only the finest musicians were invited to play at the festival. She had qualified earlier in the year and wanted to play her very best for the occasion, hence her daily practice.

There was little enough for her to do at Brook Court. Her father's housekeeper ran the house on oiled wheels. Papa saw to everything else. Except her. She had her music and books, but little else. Of course, there was always Claude to plague her hours. Emma seated herself before the harp even as she wondered if her father intended for her to accept her cousin one of these days. He made no effort to send the nodcock on his way.

The earl leaned back in his chair, tapping his foot in time to the lively music that sprang from the plucked strings of the harp. Its golden wood gleamed in the sunlight, and the delicate notes floated on the air to please the most discriminating ear. The room was soon filled with exquisite tones from the excellent instrument played by an accomplished artist.

Emma relished playing the superb Naderman harp the earl had ordered from France after the war. She also had many of Naderman's compositions. She played one now, having left the music here. It seemed she played here more than she did at home. Although her father liked to listen to a brief harp concerto in the evening from time to time, it was not something he tolerated often. She usually practiced in the mornings when Papa was off on his rounds with his agent.

The countess applauded when the music ended. The earl merely nodded his approval. Emma rejoined them in hopes of a good tea.

It was some minutes later, after the tea tray had been brought in, that the sounds of a visitor reached their ears. The little concert over, the three had gathered about the tray to enjoy the piping-hot Hyson tea and some of Cook's raspberry tarts.

Emma placed her cup on its saucer with care, then watched the wide archway with an anxious stare. What if she had been mistaken about the quality of the gentleman? She might have been so relieved to have Claude rebuffed that she had overreacted to Mr. Herbert and his fine gray eyes.

"Mr. Adam Herbert, my lord," Newton declared, his mien indicating to Emma that he highly approved of the guest.

The tall young gentleman who presented himself possessed amazing self-assurance considering he was in the vastness of the Stanwell Hall great room. Tasteful Turkish carpets were scattered over the oak floor, while the finest of furnishings filled the great room with magnificent color and texture. Emma was so accustomed to the sight she was no longer impressed by it all. But glancing about, she could see where it might intimidate a person who had not been exposed to such glory before. Evidently Mr. Adam Herbert had been around a bit.

"My lord, I am pleased to meet you," Mr. Herbert said politely. The simplicity of the statement and the lack of obvious toadying were bound to gratify the earl, who detested toads quite heartily. "I offer greetings from my father and mother."

"Well, well. So you are George's son. What brings you to this part of the world?" The earl rubbed his jaw while studying the fine specimen of English manhood before him.

"To be honest, I wished to see the area where my esteemed father grew up. I'll not deny I hoped to make your acquaintance as well—and perhaps see this venerable house. The guide books praise it highly."

"So they do," the earl complained. "Never know when some tourist—as they now call those travelers who persist in roaming about the country to see the sights—will show up at the front door wanting to be guided about the place. But I'll not be like that fellow Walpole who hides away while his cook shows Strawberry Hill to those pesky snoopers. Heard he said he ought to marry the woman, for she makes a small fortune from the viewings. Hmpf."

"Come, join us for a cup of tea," the countess invited, ignoring her husband's animadversions.

Adam had been startled to see Miss Lawrence seated so cozily with the earl and countess, partaking of tea and tarts. He wondered if she was as sharp with them as she had been to him yesterday. He doubted the earl would tolerate such behavior, judging from his talk so far.

"Thank you, I would welcome a cup of tea. This may be summer, but it's been a cool one."

The subject of the unusual weather this year occupied them for a time.

Adam listened and watched Miss Lawrence as unobtrusively as he might. She was a woman beyond mere beauty, although beautiful she surely was. She possessed a simplicity of manner that pleased him. There were no fine airs to indicate that she was accustomed to hobnobbing with an earl and his countess, particularly an earl with the reputation of Stanwell. He was known to be a high stickler. Yet she remained simple, direct, although a bit incautious.

"Do you have all you need for the Sunday school in Peetbridge, Emma?" the countess inquired when there was a lull in the conversation. She turned to Adam to add, "Our dear Emma has set up a Sunday school and takes an active role in it. She even teaches on occasion."

"Aye," the earl said, "But I do not like that she follows the tykes home to see how they are cared for. Leave that to the parson."

Adam turned an admiring pair of eyes on this amazing young woman. None of his admittedly competent sisters had actually started or led a Sunday school. What a wife she would make for some vicar! And what a pity that he could not hope for such a position, much less the money to sustain a wife and family. She looked to be accustomed to the finest in life. Adam knew enough about women's dress to know that hers was excellent quality and of recent style. She was not some poor relation, for certain.

"Indeed," the countess said, "Emma's kindness and concern is not limited to children. She keeps an eye on the elderly as well."

"And that is another bone I have to pick with you, young lady," the earl declared, wagging his finger at her. "I want a list of those old biddies you see."

Adam repressed a grin when he spotted the blush that crept over Miss Lawrence's alluring skin. Her name, Emma, had a lovely ring to it, as lovely as she was.

"Stop, please!" Miss Lawrence cried, putting forth a hand in protest. "You make me sound the veriest prig. I have so little to occupy my days, it is small wonder I need something to do. I fear I am utterly dreadful at watercolors and simply cannot embroider worth two pence. You wouldn't have me sit all day with folded hands?"

"You practice every day, my dear?" the countess asked while pouring more tea for Adam. To Adam she said, "Emma plays the harp with great skill. We are very proud of her ability. Later, she will play something for you."

"I should like that very much." Adam watched her blush deepen. Knowing his sisters, he'd wager she was not given to blushing easily. She didn't seem the sort. From her behavior at the pastry shop he'd have said she was rather rash and headstrong.

He was of a sudden extremely glad he had decided to visit Peetbridge and his great-uncle. Miss Lawrence was worth the trip all by herself.

Emma was certain her face was on fire. Why, oh *why* did the countess and the earl persist in this praise? It was as she said, she had to have something to occupy her days, and why not something that did some good instead of an insipid watercolor or a mangled piece of embroidery?

"Tell me of your family," the earl insisted. "You have five sisters, I gather?"

"Claudia is Lady Fairfax, recently widowed I'm sorry to say. Then comes Nympha, who is married to Lord Nicholas Stanhope. She is heiress to the Coxmoor fortune, and they will live part of the year in Nottinghamshire, the other near my parents on Nick's estate."

"Even I have heard of the Coxmoor wealth," the earl said, looking rather impressed.

"Priscilla is married to Earl Latimer. She met him while staying with Aunt Mercy Herbert."

"So, Mercy has taken to being a matchmaker? Hmpf."

"Drusilla is to marry the Marqess of Brentford this fall. And Tabitha is wed to Lord Latham, whose property is in Rustcombe, not far from where we live."

"Impressive, I must say," the countess remarked, looking quite surprised at the information about her great-nieces.

"Your parents have done extremely well in disposing of their daughters. What about you? What plans do you have? Are you thinking of entering the ministry as your father did?"

"Well, even if I did wish to become a parson, there simply are no vacancies available. Since retirement is something most of them disregard, not having the money upon which to live, few openings occur."

"But you say 'even if I wish,' which tells me that you are not particularly interested in that field of endeavor. What does interest you?" The earl studied his young relative with disconcerting thoroughness.

"I would like to learn land management. Perhaps I can apprentice to someone who is a bailiff or steward. It is an honorable profession."

The earl explored this topic for a time while Emma sat quietly, deep in thought. No matter that his sisters had married or were to marry very well, it seemed to her that Mr. Adam Herbert was in need of money, his father being no more than a parson. Had someone in the village revealed that she was an heiress? That she was an only child to a man who possessed great wealth? Even if she married before he died, she would have an income of five thousand pounds per annum. Upon his death she would inherit his estate, all the land and money. He had no title and there was nothing like an entail to the property. All of a sudden she was suspicious of Mr. Herbert. It was just too pat.

But the earl found no want in his great-nephew, that much was obvious. Apparently Adam Herbert passed all tests with flying colors.

Emma wanted to sniff, but knew better than to do so. She would take care in her dealings with this gentleman. It paid to be wary!

Chapter Three

"Oh, Gussie, I do not know what to think." Emma fixed her gaze on her dearest friend, Augusta Dunlop. Emma truly felt disconcerted, mixed-up. She had never encountered anyone like Adam Herbert—not that she had met that many young men. On the one hand, she was drawn to him; on the other, she was cautious.

"I shouldn't imagine a rector's son would be on the hunt for an heiress," Gussie opined. "And what makes you think anyone in Peetbridge would have had time to tell him that *you* are one. He was not there long. Thanks to you, the earl sent a footman for him the day after he arrived." Gussie frowned, seeming puzzled.

"If someone saw him escorting me into the pastry shop they might." Emma gave her friend a stubborn look. She didn't want to think ill of Mr. Herbert, but there had been a few others after her money. Of course Claude usually sent them packing, or so she learned later. He took far too much upon himself, seeing as how she would never marry *him*. She leaned back in her cozy chair where she and Gussie sat in the morning room's soft light.

The morning room at Brook Court was painted a cheerful yellow. The walls held a few of her father's favorite paintings of his horses. The girls enjoyed tea and scones.

"Well, we know Claude thinks you are his for the plucking. Since your father refuses to take you to London or even to a Salisbury assembly, let alone introduce you in Bath, perhaps you ought to think about choosing from the other gentlemen around here."

"Which is Claude, since he scares anyone else away," Emma replied with resignation.

"And now here is a relative of the earl who is not only handsome—at least from what you described—but gallant as well. And close by for the time being. Seems to me you could do far worse than settle on him." Gussie poured out another cup of tea, then sipped while watching her friend fret.

"Oh, Mr. Herbert is handsome to be sure. And well mannered, too. He handled the earl with polish. Do you know he went to Cambridge at the same time as Claude? I think he knows something about Claude. I wonder what it is?" Emma absently picked up her cup, so deep in thought she hardly attended to what she was doing.

"Your cup is empty," Gussie said with a wide grin.

"Oh. So it is. My mind is all of a dither." Emma poured herself a half-cup of tea and took a sip.

"Emma, you know that the gentleman has been visiting the earl these past few days. He has *not* come to call on you, nor has he given you much attention. How can you think him interested in you? I think you are making mountains out of molehills."

"I suppose you are right. The problem as I see it is that while I am quite able to ignore Claude until kingdom come, I don't think I could do that were Mr. Herbert to flirt with me or court me. He has a way about him." She chewed at her lip for a few moments before continuing. "Although I must say he is a bit uncivil. I *could* have handled Claude the other day. It was not necessary for Mr. Herbert to intrude as he did." Irritation flared at the remembered encounter.

"I should think it was rather nice to have a real gentleman take you away from the odious Claude." Gussie gazed off into space, a dreamy look in her blue eyes.

Emma sniffed. "Well . . ."

"I should hate to think that you are becoming too high in the instep to befriend the great-nephew of the Earl of Stanwell!" Gussie drank the last of her tea and set the cup down on its saucer with a loud click. She firmed her lips in pronounced disapproval. "You are not the only heiress in the world, you know."

"You truly think I am making too much of this?" Emma asked hesitantly. "Perhaps so. Only it is quite nasty to have suspicions of every man who looks twice at me. I know an urge to find out if he or his family is at *point-non-plus*, and an heiress is needed to set things straight."

"I don't have that problem, more's the pity," Gussie said, then gave a tragic sigh. "I have a nice dowry, but with my red hair and freckles I think I need more than what Papa allows." Her comical grimace brought a smile to Emma's face.

"Rubbish! You are slender and pretty, and those freckles are on the creamiest skin I have ever seen," Emma insisted. "Come with me this morning. I intend to go to the earl's house to practice. Papa complained that he is tired of hearing the music I plan to play at the festival whenever he comes in the house. The earl never minds." She rose from her chair and pulled her friend up, towing her along to where they could don the provincial bonnets and unadorned pelisses from last season.

Both of the girls longed to shop in fine stores, perhaps Salisbury, since London was quite beyond them. They debated the possibility of a shopping trip to Bath, knowing full well that it was as likely as London. So they fell to discussing the ways and means of managing such a thing.

Adam finished dressing, and then paused to gaze about the bedroom he had been assigned. He'd seen bedrooms at Lord Latham's house as well as fine bedrooms at Great-aunt Coxmoor's home. None could compare with the beauty of this room. It was truly an excellent chamber.

The enormous mahogany bed took pride of place, its four posts soaring toward the ceiling to be crowned with a magnificent domed canopy. The housekeeper had called it the blue bedroom. True, the walls were hung with blue silky-looking stuff. There was a nice writing table complete with all he required should he wish to write a letter home, and comfortable chairs as well. The gentleman's dressing table was of elegant design with everything needful supplied. He doubted that even Viscount Rawlinson could have been treated any better, and he, the heir.

Once he'd checked his cravat in the looking glass, he ventured forth to see what this day would hold for him. The past several days had seen a tour of the house and stables. The vastness of the buildings awed him. And to think his father had visited here often as a lad. And even more stunning was to realize that his grandfather had been brother to the present earl and grown up here. When he considered the wherewithal required to maintain such an establishment he shook his head in amazement. What a job Mr. Chambers had to steward the estate.

A lot of good it did Adam, other than allow him to visit. But he was not one to repine over what could not be helped. He ran lightly down the stairs and around to where he knew the early morning meal would be served.

"Well, my lad, are you interested in attending a local race?" the earl queried after Adam entered the breakfast room and heaped a plate with food. "There is one not too far from here tomorrow up on Marlborough downs. There will be a gold cup awarded at the end of the first day." He raised his brows at Adam in question.

"Race? Sounds promising." Adam wouldn't know a soul there and it wasn't much fun to go places alone, so his enthusiasm was restrained. He didn't think Claude Polkinghorne would welcome his company after the set-to of the other day.

"I do attend at least once a year," the earl assured him. "We shall take the landau and so have comfort. Ought to have a fine view of the course that way."

"I should deem it an honor, sir." Adam had wanted to call the earl "my lord" but quickly discovered the earl found it tiresome to be "my lorded" often. He said it was quite enough that the servants did it.

"Let's hope the good weather holds," Adam commented as he sat down to consume his meal, tucking into his food with a healthy appetite.

"After the rain of this summer it is pleasant to see the sun. Tell me, you said your sister Claudia was recently widowed. What happened?" The earl held his coffee cup before him, studying Adam over its rim.

"Lord Fairfax lost control of his horses and carriage coming home from the small town near where they live. It was very late in the evening and I gather he was a trifle foxed." Adam suspected there was more to this story than he had been told. The news had come about the time he left Rustcombe. His father had not wished him to change his plans. There was little a younger brother might do in any event, even if he had gone. His mother would go to Claudia, but Papa had to remain at home. They had been gone quite enough this year.

"Sad for a woman to be widowed so young. Children?"

"She raises his son by a previous marriage. She had no children with Lord Fairfax." Adam thought that sad, for his sister had always been fond of little ones.

"Pity, that. So, she raises the new baron. Well, at least she has a roof over her head, I imagine?" The earl leaned back in his chair to study Adam.

"Indeed. And from the sound of it, a quite acceptable one. My mother has gone to stay with her for a time."

The sound of voices in the hall reached their ears. Adam thought he recognized one of them as belonging to Miss Lawrence. He finished his coffee, then excused himself from the table. "I shall greet Miss Lawrence if that is agreeable." He would bid her good day and disappear. The lofty Miss Lawrence would have little interest in anything he might have to say.

"Fine, fine. Tell her I had the harp moved to the small drawing room. The light is just as good there and the chairs are more comfortable."

"Indeed, if Newton has not already informed her, I will be happy to relate the news." Adam barely refrained from grimacing when he heard the request. He had received the distinct impression that she found him wanting. Well, and so he was. At least he lacked the money that would be needed if one were pursuing a wife—which he wasn't, he reminded himself. Even if he found his heart's desire, he had no money with which to marry, much less have a family.

He had never thought much about the subject. But

now he had decided not to seek a position in the clergy, he had fully realized how limited his future might be. He had no taste for the military or the law. A bailiff or steward was not considered prime husband material. Best to forget anyone eligible—like Miss Lawrence, for instance.

"Mr. Herbert, you are still here."

Adam studied the two young women approaching from the vast main entry hall. One was the woman who had been on his mind just now. Not as a future wife, however. Quite the opposite. She spoke as though surprised he was still tolerated by the earl and his countess. It irritated him and he stiffened.

"Good morning. I have a message for you from the earl," he said with a slight bow. "He said the harp has been moved to the small drawing room. I believe he finds it more comfortable. He assured me that the light is just as good there as in the Great Hall." Adam took a step away.

"And so it is after the vastness of the Hall." She glanced at her friend and introduced her. "Gussie is my dearest friend. And a friend is one who will listen to me practice without complaint."

At her words, he paused politely. "I enjoy music. Perhaps I may be accounted a friend as well, for I should like to hear you play the harp." At her nod, he turned to walk along with them, wondering why in the world he hadn't escaped when he had the chance. It was obvious that Miss Lawrence could barely abide him, and he wasn't too pleased with her at the moment, either. Yet, he remained.

He wasn't quite sure which room was designated the small drawing room. The rooms all appeared large to him.

"You are finding things to interest you?" Miss Lawrence tossed him a questioning look.

Adam didn't know what she had in mind. He'd keep his answer simple. "Indeed. The house is a marvel to see. It quite excels the description my father gave me." She made no reply to his comment. They continued along the hall. Adam admired the various paintings and small tables with interesting objects on them. One could wander about this house for days and not see everything. When Miss Lawrence paused by a doorway, he found her gazing at him with a speculative gleam in her eyes.

"I suppose the earl has an activity or two planned for you?" She swept into the small drawing room. Adam followed, since she had not refused his request that he listen to her practice.

They entered a handsome room with furnishings scattered about, all of the latest style. A splendid picture of the earl and his countess with what Adam supposed was a favorite horse hung above the fireplace. Other portraits of horses hung here and there on the walls, a creamy yellow wall making a fine background for them. The clean lines of the rosewood furniture covered with green fabric were pleasing. He paused to admire a chess table done in walnut and ebony.

Miss Lawrence sat down on the chair placed before the harp. The music stand held a few sheets to which she now added more. "I need to practice and Papa is tired of listening to me. Besides, I adore coming over here."

"Tomorrow we intend to go to some race north of Marlborough." He sauntered across the room, pausing by the fireplace and listening while she tuned the harp. Was he really that fond of harp music? Or was it the harpist who intrigued him? No, not possibly. Besides, he wasn't truly interested. It would be polite to remain, however.

"Papa has a horse running in that race," Gussie said, her blue eyes flashing with interest.

"Tell me which it is and I will keep an eye on it," Adam offered, liking her fresh, open countenance.

At this point the earl joined them, having set aside his newspaper and coffee. "So . . . Dunlop has a horse in the race tomorrow."

"Indeed, my lord. Hanover is even now at the track, resting before the race." Gussie beamed a grin at him.

"Hanover, eh? Well, I suppose you plan to see him run?" The earl watched the blushing girl from beneath his brows, a slight smile tilting his lips.

"Not at all. Papa has gone and I fear I must remain at home. He would not countenance my coming along with him." Miss Dunlop seemed resigned to her fate. Undoubtedly she was left behind more often than not.

"As is only right. What goes on around the racecourse is not a proper scene for a young lady. We intend to drive over to the tracks tomorrow. We'll take a carriage and enjoy the race. Might place a few pounds on Hanover to win."

"Gussie, you truly ought to see the race." Miss Lawrence tossed a look at the earl that Adam found easy to interpret. She wanted him to include Miss Dunlop in the expedition to the races, and herself as well, most likely. He waited with watchful eyes.

"Indeed, it would be a pity if you missed it. What do you girls say to coming with us? I feel certain Mrs. Dunlop would not object. Emma—what about your father?"

"Papa is going to Salisbury to return tomorrow or the next day. I doubt he would care in any event."

There was a slightly drawn expression on her face that made Adam wonder just how kind a father Mr.

Lawrence might be. He thought that though there was a touch of defiance in her voice. Her father seemed to care little for her. Possibly it would explain her frequent visits to Stanwell Hall.

"In that event we shall plan a party. Sophia," the earl said in a carrying voice to the countess who was about to join them, "do you wish to go to the race with us tomorrow?" Adam detected a look pass between them such as he had observed between his parents, a look of communication practiced by people married some years.

"I should enjoy nothing more, dear. I will order a basket to be made up, for one can get so hungry in the fresh air. Emma, you and Gussie are to join us? And you as well, Adam?" She stood in the center of the room, hands folded before her while she assessed the young people.

Adam smiled at the thought she might be matchmaking. It almost seemed as though she might be. He gave himself a mental shake. He was becoming fanciful. It was unlikely the countess would select a young relative with little income. She'd be a fool to think about such a thing, and certainly no friend to Miss Lawrence. That Miss Dunlop didn't so much as enter his mind didn't occur to him.

Newton paused at the doorway. "Mr. Polkinghorne to see you, my lord."

Claude hadn't waited as proper. He entered the room on Newton's heels. "Good day, sir. I thought to see how your guest goes on."

"I think he does quite well," the earl replied, a quizzical look in his eyes. They passed the time of day, chatting about the fine weather and prospects for next day.

"I expect you plan to take in the race tomorrow. I

know you always attend." Claude sauntered close to where Emma Lawrence sat poised by the harp. Adam thought she looked anything but pleased to see her cousin.

"Indeed, we are making up a party to go early in the morning. Are you planning to go?"

Adam stepped back to lean against the fireplace mantel while watching Claude's maneuvering. Were he a betting man, he'd wager that Claude wanted to go with them and wondered how the scoundrel would manage to accomplish the trick.

"Well, my carriage needs a wheel repaired. I am afraid that no matter how much I would like to go, I cannot."

"Of course you must join our party," the earl said with cool politeness.

"Dear, that will require another carriage. The landau cannot take six in comfort," the countess said in the quietest of voices. "The three young people might be on one side, but with you and I on the other . . ." her voice trailed off while she looked in Adam in expectation.

"Why don't Claude and I come along in my carriage?" Adam offered, knowing full well it was what the countess counted upon. "Then no one will be inconvenienced."

Claude did not look delighted with the offer. However, seeing that he couldn't push his way into the earl's carriage, he conceded defeat. "Thank you, Herbert. Much obliged. What time do you intend to leave in the morning?"

The earl decided the time and other details. Before long Claude bowed his way from the room, looking annoyed because he knew full well that Adam could and would remain.

The countess walked to stand by Emma Lawrence. "I trust this does not distress you, my dear."

Emma shook her head. "What could you do with Claude hinting so obviously. The earl is such a dear man, so polite. I believe it would grieve him to cause anyone the slightest distress—even Claude. What a pity my cousin chose this morning to descend upon you. One would think he anticipated such a plan on your part."

"Well, you heard Claude say he knew we always went," the countess concluded before drifting off, murmuring something about consulting with Cook in regards to the basket of lunch for the next day.

The earl joined Adam to stand by the fireplace. Even on a summery day there was a small fire burning to take any damp from the room. He poked at it, then straightened to look at Adam. "Thank you, dear boy, for taking the difficulty from our outing tomorrow. I suspect, upon reflection, that Emma and Claude would be at daggers drawn before we reached the racecourse. Pity they cannot get along better. You said you went to Cambridge with him."

Adam responded to the question that hung in the air between them. "I fear that Polkinghorne did not have the most savory of reputations, sir."

"Local girls?" the earl softly inquired, with a knowing look on his face.

"Indeed, sir." Adam had no wish to be tattling tales, but on the other hand it seemed imperative that the earl understand that Claude went far beyond the usual. The girls he assaulted were left with bitter memories. "His victims required long periods of convalescence." He spoke quietly, not wishing his words to be overheard by Miss Lawrence.

The earl looked pensive, then sighed. "Bad, very bad. He'll not do for our Emma in that event."

"I should think not, sir." As to what sort of man would do for the rash young lady, Adam couldn't say. He rather envied the fellow in any event.

Chapter Four

The carriages stood in the stable yard and horses had been put to. The usual noise, when an expedition of this sort begins, could be heard—the harness jingling, grooms muttering, the coachman issuing last-minute orders. A footman stowed the hamper of food neatly behind the coachman's seat.

Adam didn't relish the trip, unhappily assigned to a two-hour drive with Claude for company. He went to stand by his cabriolet. To his surprise it was well polished, evidence of the care given by the staff in the coach house.

He was surprised the earl preferred a landau to travel in rather than a coach, then recalled the intention he had of reclining therein while they watched the races.

He never knew quite how she managed it, but the countess walked up with a silent Miss Lawrence firmly in tow. Emma wore a reluctant expression.

"I believe it would be nice for dear Emma to drive with you. I do not think she has ever had the pleasure of driving in a cabriolet. They are such dashing vehicles. I'm sure you will both agree it is an admirable plan. Claude will drive with us." She didn't wait for a reply, merely walked over to be assisted into the earl's fine vehicle, leaving Miss Lawrence unable to argue but obviously displeased.

Miss Lawrence's eyes flashed with annoyance, Adam noted with amusement. He'd wager had she been able she would have refused to ride with him. The countess had effectively cut her off, leaving the beautiful Miss Lawrence fuming silently. He wondered how long that would last.

The groom assisted the young lady into the cabriolet while Adam took the reins in hand and settled on his side of the carriage. He glanced sideways to note her hands were clenched in her lap. Well, he might enjoy the drive, but she clearly wanted no part of him or his cabriolet. At least it would be better than having Claude next to him.

Claude strode up to the carriage, his face cold with fury. "Dash it all, Herbert, ain't that a bit of brass?"

Adam gave him a smile. "The countess suggested Miss Lawrence would enjoy a drive in the cabriolet."

"Enjoy the dust! Ha!" Claude spun around and climbed into the landau with an air of hauteur that ill became him.

"He has a point, you know," Adam felt obliged to say. "We shall have to keep back a little to avoid eating their dust. I trust you will not find it too annoying."

She gave him a surprised look but said nothing before turning away again. All he could see was the profile of a fetching bonnet. Somehow even her bonnet looked annoyed.

Adam resigned himself to the tedium of hours of silence while managing his horse and coping with the necessary changes on the route.

The roads north were not in too bad a condition. They left the estate and Peetbridge to cross the Avon before joining the main road to Marlborough. With a fast change of horses at an inn on the edge of Pewsey, they made excellent time. Adam was impressed with the quality of his job horse.

He commented on the fine cattle in the fields they passed. The rolling green fields were ideal for them. Further south he had seen sheep dotted across the downs.

Miss Lawrence unbent enough to exclaim with delight at the masses of harebells and white campion seen along the hedge banks here and there.

"You like flowers?" Adam inquired, happy to find something that pleased the silent young woman at his side. The air seemed to hum between them. He supposed it was her hostility. He doubted that the sensation was the pull of attraction, since she had made her dislike of him obvious. To him, at least. The countess seemed oblivious to the constraint. He glanced at his companion, glad that all he was required to do was to follow the earl's carriage.

"I do," she said at long last. "Although Papa says it is nonsense to bother with planting flowers, I enjoy them." She turned her head, enabling him to view her face.

"Well, I daresay he permits a few beds of flowers to please you. Otherwise, I should think you could manage to work in a few plants in the kitchen garden."

"I have no flowerbeds, but that is a very good idea. Thank you for suggesting it." She looked surprised.

Did she think him lost to any interest in a garden or consigned to only masculine pursuits?

"I shall take over a small part of the kitchen garden next spring," she continued. "With just the two of us, and Papa never entertaining much, other than a few cronies, we do not need what we once did."

"You live a rather solitary life, I gather?" he said.

"That is why I am so often at the earl's home. They are so kind to me. With no granddaughters, they somewhat adopted me." She gave a little laugh, clenching her fingers in that nervous little gesture she made earlier.

Adam considered that laugh a trifle forced and wondered at the kind of man who could ignore his daughter.

The approach to Marlborough brought an increase in travelers on the road. Likely most were going to Bath, possibly to London, but a goodly number were headed north to where the racecourse was located on the road to Rockley.

"High Street is set on the slope of a hill and has St. Peter's church at one end with St. Mary's at the other," Miss Lawrence said, evidently thinking she needed to say something. The broad street bustled with vehicles going every direction. Many carriages had stopped for a change of cattle.

The earl insisted they must pause at the Castle Inn, famed for its hospitality. When they arrived, they found the place swarming with inn servants, waiters, grooms, and footmen. Adam was impressed with its green lawns. Few inns he had seen possessed so pleasant an aspect.

As he assisted Miss Lawrence from the cabriolet, she gazed up at the fine inn. "This was once the home of the Countess of Hertford," she declared. "The Northumberlands sold it when they inherited the place. How distressed she must have been to see it so." She accepted the glass of lemonade brought to her, then placed the empty glass on the tray in the other vehicle. She tugged at Adam's arm.

"Come, walk around here with me," Emma urged. "Some boys cut the image of a white horse in the chalk on Granham Hill. Oh, it's not as large or as old as some others, but good enough to be spared a look." She pulled him along with her.

Adam was curious to see the White Horse, but he was intrigued how Emma Lawrence had literally come to life upon reaching the town. She almost danced along the one side of the broad street, reaching out to tug his arm, urging him to hurry.

It wasn't huge, but large enough. "Impressive."

"There! I thought you might like to see it. We have a great number of unusual sights in this area. I suppose you have such where you live as well? In Kent, I believe the countess said?" Rather than gaze at the oddly shaped white horse that had been cut into the chalk hill-side, she turned to study him.

Conscious of her scrutiny, Adam ignored the curious sight to face her. "Well? Have you reached a decision?"

"I do not know what you are talking about." Her eyes took on a suspicious gleam. "A decision about what?"

"You know full well that you have held me in aversion, even suspicion, ever since we met. I can't think why."

A faint rose color crept over her cheeks. "Rubbish. Err— I mislike your attitude to me. I do not need to be defended from every paltry thing."

"I am unaware that I have *interfered* with your life in any way—although perhaps someone should. When did I ever?"

"I will have you know that I can handle my cousin without intercession from anyone. He is annoying, a truly vexing creature, but I do not believe he would ever truly harm me." She sniffed.

Adam thought of what he personally knew of Claude's character and grimaced. "So be it, then. But do not say you were not warned of his character by me."

"I should like to know what it is that has turned you against Claude." She was cajoling him to tell her what he felt she best not know. How could he reveal to a gently reared young woman the sorts of behavior Claude had indulged in while at school?

"No," Adam replied, more sharply than he intended.

"You have nothing on him." Emma dismissed Adam's tone. Inwardly she admitted she detested her cousin. She had wanted to learn what Mr. Herbert knew about him so she could use it as an argument in the event her father decided that she should marry Claude. She would do almost anything to avoid that fate.

Adam was sorely tried at this point. He had wished to be the gentleman with this impulsive young woman, but she pushed to the limit. "There are some things you are better off not knowing." There was no way he would reveal the truth. He'd told the earl some, but not all of it. Whether she realized it or not, the madcap did need protection from her cousin. And, although he was dismayed at her attitude, he would see that she was sheltered while he was able, in spite of what he'd told her.

"How tantalizing you are," she said, clearly disappointed.

Adam lightly touched her arm, feeling a strange desire assail him, a desire quite at odds with her fierce rejection of him. He wanted to kiss those scornful lips, crush Miss Lawrence to his chest. She was a fetching armful, even if she was a spitfire.

Tension lingered in the air until his good sense prevailed and he put aside his peculiar notions.

"I believe the groom is looking for us," Adam said, relieved to end the situation that promised to get out of hand with this hot-tempered young woman.

She shook herself free and, head high, began to march back to where the carriages waited for them. When Adam realized she was about to step in a puddle, he took her arm again, guiding her around it. "When you walk with your nose in the air, you may find yourself in trouble."

"I do not like you, Mr. Herbert."

"Why? Because I refuse to put up with your nonsense? Come, get into the carriage and we can be on our way. It may be early, but I fancy the earl is eager to reach the racecourse." She allowed him to hand her up, but other than muted thanks, said nothing more.

She retreated into silence again, and Adam wondered if it was to be thus the rest of the day. "Miss Dunlop seems an agreeable person," he commented as they wound their way through the throng of carriages and headed north again. Soon the River Kennet was behind them and the cabriolet kept pace with the landau.

"Pity the countess didn't push *her* at your cabriolet. I daresay she has never ridden in one before either."

"Well, I will be happy to offer her the opportunity, you may be sure. No doubt it will afford me more pleasure than the termagant who rides with me presently," Adam declared, thoroughly fed up with the beautiful Miss Lawrence at the moment.

"How dare you speak so to me! Why, of all the nerve!"

"My dear Miss Lawrence, you would be amazed at the things I dare to do. May I suggest you take a more conciliatory path? Otherwise, I might be tempted to do what your governess so obviously failed to accomplish. I am told paddling is most salutary!" Adam snapped at her, quite at the point where he was ready to do as he threatened.

"Of all the unspeakable persons! I doubt the countess has the least idea of the manner of man she foisted upon me." Emma was so furious that Adam could feel her anger as they jounced over a piece of rough road.

"I do beg your pardon, but I believe she foisted you

upon me, truth be told. However, I made no objection—then. I thought you superior company to your wicked cousin."

"Oh!" she exclaimed in patent exasperation.

He saw they had reached the racecourse. He judged it to be about a mile in length and roughly parallel to the road that eventually led to the village of Rockley. What a good thing he had studied the earl's map last evening. Not that it was a particularly good map, but it did have the local places on it.

"Thanks be, we are here!" Miss Lawrence said, gathering her skirts in preparation to quitting the carriage.

A groom ran up to take the horse while Adam jumped down and strode around to reach the other side of the vehicle in time to help his companion. He placed his hands to either side of her slim waist and held her a few moments longer than strictly necessary, smiling up into her annoyed face.

What a pity she was such a prickly creature. She was beautiful, her lively countenance making her an object of envy for many a girl, he was certain.

"Put me down!" she whispered, mindful of the others far too close to permit chastising him as he was sure she wanted to do.

Adam gently lowered her until her feet found the ground. She frowned up at him, a hint of bewilderment in her eyes. "I do believe you *like* to aggravate me."

"It beats silence." Adam laughed as she gave him a scathing look before marching away to join Miss Dunlop.

Adam dismissed her from his mind and crossed to where the earl beckoned him.

"Well," Gussie asked quietly, "how was the journey in the cabriolet? You do not appear pleased by it, Emma."

Emma glanced back at the tall, handsome gentleman whose patience she knew she had severely tried. "He is an exasperating man."

"Well, cuz, what think you of cabriolets now you have suffered a trip in one?" Claude asked as he swaggered up to join her and Gussie. "I daresay he was cow-handed and used his poor horse ill. Sorry sort of vehicle, I'd say."

"And you have seen so many cabriolets, I suppose," Emma said evenly, wishing him gone.

"More than a few," he replied with a superior smile, the kind that raised her temper.

"He handled the horse just as he ought—which is more than I can say for you, Claude. It seems a fine carriage, built so that it can be pulled by one horse and hold two people comfortably. It even has a windscreen in addition to the leather apron to protect against bad weather. I thought it quite handsome."

"Just hope it doesn't rain!" He laughed, evidently thinking himself a wit.

Emma turned her back on him, urging Gussie to walk with her. "Oh, how he annoys me."

"If he annoys you and the handsome Mr. Herbert is exasperating, I think you are difficult to please," Gussie said with a grin.

"Claude is a mere nothing. Mr. Herbert is another matter. He—"

Whatever she was about to confess to Gussie was set aside for the moment when the earl called them to his side.

"You ladies may sit up here with Sophie. I'll take Adam—and Claude, too, if he wants—closer to the racecourse. We want to look over the horses."

Emma watched them walk away, turning suddenly to the countess to say, "I wish there was an assembly this evening. It is too bad of them to discontinue them. Papa said they intend to have the races elsewhere next year."

"Chippenham or Burderop, I gather," the countess said with a brisk nod. "That is the way it goes, my dear. But . . . perhaps you will be somewhere else by then. Did you enjoy your cabriolet ride?"

"Perhaps there was too much dust?" Gussie wondered.

"There were pretty flowers along the road. Did you notice them?" Emma said by way of a reply. For some reason she was disinclined to discuss the trip. But she would make certain she did not return with him. Or perhaps she would, just to plague the man.

"You are not answering my question, dear. What meaning must I attach to that, pray tell?" the countess asked, her voice full of innuendo.

"Do not, I beg you, play the matchmaker for me." Emma looked to her lap, where her hands clutched each other as they had on the drive.

"Dear, I am concerned about you," the countess said gently. She adjusted her parasol to ward off the sun. "Your father shows no sign of finding you a husband. You may have to find your own. How often does a handsome young gentleman come our way? I think our great-nephew a good man, well raised by his equally good parents. We should welcome the connection." She opened her mouth as though to add to this, then apparently thought better of it. "Look, there is Hanover! How gallant he looks. Such a fine horse."

Emma stood up, resting one hand on the side of the landau. "The view is not the best here. Excuse me, I want to see Hanover." She quickly left the carriage, ignoring the mild protest from the countess. The proper

Gussie remained. Emma ought not leave, but something compelled her.

Threading her way through the throng of people—mostly men, she realized—she hunted for Gussie's father. Instead she bumped into the odious Claude, who immediately grasped her arm. He held it just tight enough so she couldn't escape.

"Well, pretty cousin, you escaped Lady Stanwell's eye for the moment?" He glanced over her head to the landau before returning his attention to Emma.

"There is no need to grab my arm, Claude. I can manage well without *your* regard." Even with the press of people all around them, Emma felt a moment of panic. Why, she wasn't sure, but Claude had a most peculiar look in his eyes. She didn't trust that look.

"Let us take a little stroll, dear cousin mine. The racecourse spreads over some very pretty country. You can see the winning post up there at the high end of it. Come."

Emma dug in the heels of her half-boots, thankful she had worn something more sensible than the blue Morocco slippers she had been tempted to put on. "I will go nowhere with you, Claude. I cannot imagine why you think I wish for your company. I want to see Hanover. Look, Haggitt is up on him and walking him round to keep his muscles warmed." She broke free of Claude's grasp and darted away from him. When she glanced back to see if he followed, she collided with a sturdy figure of a man. She grabbed at his coat to keep from falling, only to find herself pulled tightly against a well-muscled body.

"Well, I didn't think you would seek me out in such a manner. Come to apologize, my dear madcap?"

"Mr. Herbert!" Emma closed her eyes in frustration.

"Really, my girl, you do need a keeper." He looked

back to encounter Claude's glare. "Or is your cousin annoying you again? Tell me, who irks you more—Claude or me?"

"Both!" She gulped, unwilling to admit how welcome his strong arms and manly chest were after escaping from Claude's clutches. Adam Herbert gently guided her to the front of him, where she had an excellent view of the course. When he kept her close against him in an oddly protective gesture, she didn't protest.

A bay filly ran to win the first of the races. Afterwards the group gathered by the landau to enjoy the picnic sent along for them.

Emma felt confused. Why, as much as she disliked the man, had she felt so safe when Mr. Herbert stood behind her? Protected, that was it, she decided as she munched her way through a sandwich.

Mr. Herbert offered her some of what the earl said was home-brewed cider. Thirsty, for it had been somewhat dusty on the road, she drank deeply. She finished her sandwich, then held her glass out for more cider. The sun was warm and there was little wind.

Adam, after one mug of the cider, decided prudence the best course. It had a kick to it and home-brewed cider could be lethal drink. He wondered if Miss Emma Lawrence was aware of how flushed she had become. He knew better than to caution her. That would really bring her wrath down on his head.

The trip home ought to be very interesting. But first they had to finish the races. It should be a delightful day.

He heard a faint hiccup and repressed a grin. Oh, it definitely was going to be an entertaining day.

Chapter Five

Emma cast a defiant look at Mr. Herbert. His eyes reproved her. What right did he have to censure her in any way? She did not understand why *he* should disturb her so. She replaced her glass with care, then flounced away from the landau, quite ignoring the concerned look given her by the countess.

"Emma . . ." The countess cautioned. "Do be careful."

Emma continued on her way, undeterred by prudence.

"May I assist you, Miss Lawrence?" The voice came from the man who had joined her in her pursuit of a place near the racecourse. "You ought not be alone."

She could feel his presence at her side and she knew who it was without looking. "I shall be quite fine, Mr. Herbert." Unfortunately, she stumbled at this point. He probably took delight in helping her stay on her feet. He tucked a hand under her arm, steadying her with a nicety of manner.

"The ground is a little uneven here. Please permit my assistance, Miss Lawrence." His touch lightly guided her. It also sent a tremor of sensation leaping through her arm to the rest of her body. She shouldn't have drunk that cider! She now recalled Papa saying that the earl's home-brewed cider was very strong. She told herself it couldn't have much effect on her.

Mr. Herbert was so terribly polite she simply couldn't be rude to the man, even if she didn't particularly like him. She wished, however, to make it perfectly clear that she did not need him or his help.

"Sir," she said politely, "I am well able to cope." Her civil avowal was rather spoiled by a faint hiccup.

Fortunately for him, he said not a word. A dagger glance revealed that an attractive smile lurked about that firm mouth. She best beware of him. It would never do for her to actually like the gentleman!

The next race was about to begin. Mr. Herbert escorted her to the edge of the course where a low fence restrained the attendees from straying into the path of the racehorses.

"Do you recognize any of the horses that are to run?" he asked, bending close so he might be heard over the general noise.

Emma shrugged. "Not really. I merely like to see them race. It is such a challenge." A part of her welcomed the solid gentleman who stood behind her. She was not so green that she didn't know it was not the thing for a young woman to be here alone. She invited trouble.

Next to them she could hear a cluster of racing notables discussing the points of several horses lining up for the race. They speculated on odds, hotly debating one horse over another.

Their conversation came to an abrupt end at the signaling of the imminent start of the next race.

There was a moment of soundless expectancy. Sparrows chirped in a nearby bush. The soft sigh of the wind on the downs brought the harsh *churr* of a starling as it noisily flew overhead. All those who watched felt the tension.

Then the steward's handkerchief fell and they were

off. Shouts of encouragement followed them. Emma cheered with no particular horse favored.

A goodly number of enthusiasts rode along just out of the way from one vantage point to the next so as not to miss one moment of the thrill of the race.

Emma accepted the spyglass her escort handed her in time to see the winner crossing the line at the winning post. "When does Hanover run, I wonder?" she queried as she returned the glass.

"I would ask, but I'd not leave you alone here in the press of the crowd." Again he supported her with the slightest of touch. Slight it might be, she was highly conscious of it.

Emma was about to inform him that she could manage quite well, when a drunken chap bumped against her, begging her pardon in a slurred voice.

"See what I mean, my dear?"

"I am not your *dear* anything," she said in a frigid voice, turning to stare up at him. He was a fair way up, too, being taller than the odious Claude. His look of amusement didn't set well with her. "I believe it might be well to move along the fence. As you said, the press of the crowd is to be avoided." Her head swam slightly as she spun about. She really would have to watch the ground, for it seemed extremely uneven.

Aware Mr. Herbert was at the moment studying the winning horse that was parading along the fence, Emma saw her chance to gain her freedom. Precisely why it was so important to be independent of him, she couldn't have said.

She lurched forward—that grass really ought to have been scythed—and then regained her balance, sauntering away from him along the fence until she reached the point not too distant where the fence ended. From here on the attendees were on their own to keep out of the path of the horses when they ran.

In a rather pleasant haze, she looked back to see where the horses assembled for the next race. A fine assortment appeared in the lineup, and Emma stepped forward to get a better view.

Just as the handkerchief dropped, that same boozy man bumped into her, pushing her into the path of the oncoming horses. She froze. Not even the awareness she was in danger could move her.

Suddenly she was swept off her feet, knocked sideways, and dragged back out of the path of the nearest horse. It raced past in a blur of gray.

Every muscle and quite a few bones in her body protested this Turkish treatment. Then she became aware of his body atop hers. Those protesting muscles responded to the feel of him, noting how well they fit together. How strange, to sense such an intimate connection, yet be fully clothed. Through her delicate sprigged muslin and apricot spencer she could feel where the lines of his blue coat pressed against her. His boots were beyond her and for that she could only be thankful. It was enough to have that firm form sprawled over her.

Mr. Herbert drew back a moment, his gray eyes watching her, his hands to either side of her body, close, far too close.

Warmth surged through her that had nothing to do with the temperature of the day. She knew the wildest desire to wrap her arms about him, embrace him. A warning rang in her head. A young lady simply did not behave like this. Particularly in public!

Stunned, she slowly disentangled herself from the gentleman who lay half across her. Mr. Herbert rolled to one side while she slowly sat up. A glance around informed her that quite a few people gathered close by, offering words of advice and comfort, and she also noticed some scandalized looks from nearby women.

Her bonnet was askew, her pretty dress soiled, and heaven only knew where her reticule had gone! She glared at the man who had been stretched across her.

"I might have known it was you! Mr. Herbert, I told you before that I could take care of myself."

He gave her a grim smile that had the most peculiar effect on her senses. Firmly pushing aside that strange notion, she continued to glare at the most aggravating man she had ever met.

Rather than reply, he rose, reached out to straighten her bonnet, found her reticule, then helped her up. She reluctantly accepted his hand in rising. When firmly on her feet, she met his stern gaze with inner trepidation. She didn't think she had ever seen a man so angry with her. Those other fortune-hunters seemed to think she could do no wrong. This man was different.

"I beg to disagree, Miss Lawrence," he snapped at her. "Had I not acted with promptitude, you would now be dead." His look of scorn cut to her heart. "You little fool, what possessed you to do such a thing? How much better it would have been for you to remain with the countess in the landau."

The cold expression he wore was enough to sear her heart. He was wrong! She wasn't a fool!

The people clustered around began to drift away, since nothing more was forthcoming. Ignoring the few who remained, he left her! She didn't even have a chance to explain, not that she could have thought of two words that would help. He left her alone—just as she had insisted he do. She wasn't sure she welcomed it.

She stood for a few moments before attempting to return to the carriage. Alone, she discovered that she was fair game for the roistering crowd of men. A glance told her that the proper women who attended were perched in their carriages in complete safety. She was virtually the sole woman along the fence, save for a few who were obviously no better than they should be. She closed her eyes in utter humiliation.

"What say, dearie? Care to join me in a leetle celebration?" The bosky man lurched against her, sending fumes of beer and brandy wafting in her direction even as he slid his arm about her waist.

With great determination, she wrenched away from his hold and marched up the slope to where the countess stared at her with a shocked expression.

The groom opened the door to the landau and assisted a much-chastened Emma into the carriage.

"Emma, I cannot believe what I just saw. How could you jeopardize your reputation in such a hoydenish manner?"

The scolding from a woman she loved so much was even worse than the scorn heaped on her head by Mr. Herbert. Emma fought back the tears that longed to flow.

"I wished to see better." It was a lame excuse at best, but it was all she could summon to her confused mind.

"I think you had better remain with us from now on," the countess advised. "You can see almost as well from here and there will be no danger of being accosted by drunken men! Heaven only knows what the gossips will say. And never think that men do not do such. They are worse than women!"

Emma sat in humble silence as the countess went on to read her a scold such as she had not endured since she was a small and rather naughty child.

Emma also observed that Mr. Herbert kept his distance. Only Claude drew near to utter the most awful drivel, words of sympathy intermixed with condemnation of Herbert for placing her in such a position.

Finally Emma gave her cousin a direct look. "To be fair, it was not Mr. Herbert's fault. He tried to dissuade me from going past the fence. That he acted quickly without thought for his own safety is to his everlasting credit."

Claude protested, although it seemed weak.

"Cousin, I would have been dead now had it not been for Mr. Herbert and you should know it." It occurred to her in a flash of comprehension that if she died, Claude would be heir to the fortune . . . unless Papa left it elsewhere in his will. She'd overlooked that rather significant bit of intelligence.

Gussie moved closer to Emma. "Pay no heed to him, Emma. You know how little sense he has."

Claude stalked off in high dudgeon. Within a few minutes Emma observed him in conversation with one of the notables she had seen earlier.

"When does Hanover race? Will it be for the gold plate?" Emma hoped to deflect the talk from her debacle.

"Indeed, that is what Papa hopes." Gussie gave Emma a consoling pat. "Are you feeling better now? I felt so sorry for you when Mr. Herbert returned and you stayed behind."

Emma gave her friend an appreciative look. How nice it was to have friends who didn't leap to condemn one. "I'll confess that it is good to be quietly seated."

"You do not fear being labeled a madcap? I heard that word bandied about by a few gentlemen who were close to the carriage." Fortunately, Gussie spoke softly.

"The men Claude is speaking with now?" Emma

gave her cousin a scornful look. Inwardly she shrunk from the label he wanted to paste on her. Madcap? No, she couldn't be that, surely. Merely because she wanted to see a bit better? But, a wee voice in the back of her head reminded, she could have borrowed the spyglass belonging to Mr. Herbert and seen as well. And she wouldn't have been in danger from the horses or that bosky man. . . .

"Mr. Herbert saved your life, did he not?" Gussie said breathlessly. The admiring look she bestowed on that gentleman caused Emma's stomach to lurch.

"To be fair, he did. But I would have been fine if that idiotish man hadn't pushed me onto the course."

"Isn't he the same man Claude is talking to at this moment?" Gussie turned around just enough so she could take a second look.

Emma peered around her friend to see for herself.

"Indeed. Trust him to speak to someone so disreputable." She sniffed with disdain.

Not much later Mr. Herbert appeared at the carriage once again, this time to speak quietly with the countess. They looked at Emma from time to time, and she would have given a great deal to know what was being said. With the noise from the crowd and horses, it was impossible to overhear a word.

When he had departed, Emma shifted to the other side of the carriage and next to the countess. "Is there something amiss?"

"You may as well know that the sprawl you and Mr. Herbert took earlier is the talk of the afternoon. That the daughter of the wealthy Mr. Lawrence was seen on the grass with a gentleman draped across her is a delicious tidbit. You may be certain it will be carried back to the various houses come the end of the day. What a blessing we do not plan to remain overnight for tomorrow's race. I doubt you would have a shred of reputation left, my dear."

Emma studied the face of the woman she deemed near a mother and shrank against the squabs. "Is it truly so bad?"

"Worse. May I suggest you not leave the carriage for the rest of the afternoon?" Her gaze was unrelenting and she sounded more than serious. She sounded grim.

Emma nodded. She gave the bottle of cider a baleful look before turning her attention to the next race.

"Hanover is up next. Mr. Herbert gave me his glass. Come and you can see how fine our horse looks," Gussie cried with enthusiasm.

Offering a contrite mien to the countess, Emma slipped over to sit by her good friend. She accepted the spyglass and took an obedient look at Hanover. There was no gainsaying that he was a handsome horse. His chestnut coat gleamed in the sun, and he tossed his head as though warning the others that he was a horse to be reckoned with.

"Well, Grandmother! I scarce thought to find you here. But then I should have recalled that Stanwell never misses the first day of these races. It has been excellent, has it not?" Viscount Rawlinson positioned his cabriolet close to the landau so he might chat with his relative without the necessity of leaving his carriage.

"Rawlinson! What a surprise! I never expected to see you here!" the countess exclaimed. "As to it being an excellent race, there are some who might disagree with you on that." Her gaze strayed to where Emma Lawrence confided in her dearest friend.

"Who's with Emma?" Having known each other since their early years, there was little formality and absolutely no love between Emma and Rawlinson.

"I cannot believe you haven't met her. Augusta Dunlop is Emma's bosom friend. Gussie," she said, raising her voice to be heard, "haven't you met our grandson, Viscount Rawlinson?"

Gussie shyly shook her head and blushed. "I am happy to meet you, sir." The sprinkling of freckles stood out on her delicate ivory skin. Her blue eyes sparkled with delight in the day. The pale blue parasol tilted over her shoulder proved an appealing contrast to her vibrant hair.

"Good grief, a country charmer," the viscount murmured. He bowed as well as he could, given he had the control of a mettlesome horse before his carriage. "I am most pleased to make your acquaintance. Anyone who can tolerate my brat of a neighbor is to be highly commended."

"Rawlinson," the countess cautioned. "Not today, I beg you." She met his gaze with raised brows and a faint nod.

"Emma in hot water, is she?" He lowered his voice, but kept an eye on her.

"Worse. Mr. Herbert—our great-nephew and something of a cousin to you—dragged her out of the path of the racing horses and in the process pulled her to the ground. Her bonnet was askew, and I don't know what all else befell her. *But* he was draped across her while both of them were on the ground. True, he saved her life, but in such a manner!" She touched her grandson lightly on his arm, her eyes revealing the seriousness of the situation. "I am very concerned. With no mother to guide her, she falls into scrapes far too often. And her father . . . well, the less said about him, the better. I have yet to decide what we shall do in regards to driving home later on."

"Good heavens!" Rawlinson cast another look at Emma Lawrence and shook his head. "Too headstrong by half. What can you do? It sounds as though she has truly done it this time."

"There is little to be said at the moment, but you know gossips. I'll consult with Stanwell later. He is over there near the starting point with Mr. Dunlop and Adam Herbert. Dunlop has a horse set to run in the next race. Hanover."

"No! Really? Miss Dunlop's father bred that amazing animal? How interesting. I must get to know her better." With a flick of his reins, the viscount was off to draw his vehicle close to the fence so he could observe the famous Hanover in his run for the gold plate.

Emma watched the Stanwell heir move his vehicle into position. "I cannot believe Rawlinson is here." She looked at the countess, adding, "Did you have the least notion he might attend, ma'am?"

"Not the slightest. He usually never leaves London. I wonder what brought him here at this time of year?"

"Perhaps the races?" Gussie suggested.

"Perhaps." The countess watched her grandson chat with Mr. Dunlop and the earl. Mr. Herbert joined them and the four men looked to be in deep conversation. "I would give more than a little to know what is being said."

"Hush, the race is about to begin," Emma admonished. Not that she was obsessed with the race, far from it now. She made a fervent prayer that she might scrape through this incident without any serious damage. The aches from her rude shove to the ground were the least of her problems.

Horses could be seen gathering at the starting post. There was that moment of tense silence as they lined up. Again the handkerchief fell and they were off, with Hanover setting the pace. Haggitt wore Dunlop's colors of silvery blue, which stood out against the gleam of the chestnut's coat.

Gussie stood to watch as Hanover thundered along the mile-long course. He was a blur of chestnut fire, Haggitt urging him on. The promise of the gold plate spurred the jockeys up the course. The sound of a dozen horses pounding the turf as they headed for the final stretch leading up to the winning post floated back to tease their ears.

"Hanover is neck and neck with another horse—Blaze, I think," Gussie reported, not offering the spyglass to the others. She bounced on the seat, about as close as Gussie ever came to behaving with impropriety. "He is closing in on the post. Oh! He has won!" She lowered the glasses and gave the countess and Emma a triumphant grin. "Oh, I say, that was utterly wonderful! I am so glad I am here to see it! Papa will be so very pleased." She gave another little bounce before settling demurely on the seat of the landau.

Mr. Dunlop went to meet his prime horse, and as they walked toward the cluster of people by the starting post he could be seen talking earnestly with his jockey. There was an air of jubilance about them.

"Mama will be so happy. I think we are all a little horse-mad in our family," Gussie confessed.

Emma looked over the heads of the fashionables and other horse-mad people to where she spotted the earl, the viscount, and Mr. Herbert welcoming Mr. Dunlop and Hanover, with Haggitt still astride.

As she watched, Mr. Herbert turned to look her way. She couldn't make out his expression, but it chilled her heart when he spun away from her. It was as though he couldn't bear to so much as look at her.

Shortly after, the earl appeared at the landau, offering his wife a look that apparently told her much. "We will leave now. Haggitt said he feels it will rain. Best return home before that."

Emma's mouth was dry, her heart beating erratically. Would she remain in the landau? Or would Mr. Herbert welcome her back into his cabriolet? She waited, her hands folded, clutching one another in dread.

"We shall return as we came, I believe," the earl concluded.

Within minutes everyone rearranged themselves. Gussie was taken up with the viscount, who was full of talk about her father and Hanover.

Emma faced Mr. Herbert.

"Come, we are deemed to be close friends. Smile at me." His own smile was a trifle strained but would look genuine at a distance.

"How quaint!" But, much chastened, Emma smiled.

Chapter Six

More than a few people stared at Emma as Mr. Herbert assisted her into his fine cabriolet. Gentlemen could be seen leaning against the carriages that sat here and there along the edge of the racecourse. They were relaying something, to be certain. And since most people looked her way, Emma knew it had to do with her supposedly scandalous behavior. She pretended not to care. If those people had nothing better to do than to gossip about what had happened, there was little if anything she could do about it.

She brushed down her sprigged muslin, straightened the apricot spencer, and fingered the ribands that tied her neat little bonnet. She would have to do until she might get home again and change.

Let them gossip and eye her with their narrowed scrutiny. She had fallen—been pushed, to be accurate. Mr. Herbert rushed to rescue her, propelling her to the ground to save her life. Why should such a thing be a scandal? Merely because he ended up sprawled across her in a most shocking position was not *totally* beyond the pale. After all, he *had* saved her. Yet she found it difficult to maintain her composure.

"Ignore those who stare, Miss Lawrence," her escort advised. "Act like the countess and pretend you do not notice anything unusual."

"Why couldn't someone put it around how you saved my life and they could praise you as my hero?" Emma watched as he checked the harness, then joined her in the carriage. "For you are," she added in all fairness. Foolish though she might be, she was honest to a fault when pressed.

His face reddened slightly but he said nothing.

"Mr. Herbert, what did the earl decide? Apparently something was said when you all met at the starting point." She had to know what had been determined. After all, it was her reputation at stake.

"He mentioned to the group around him that he was much obliged to me for saving you from certain demise," Mr. Herbert replied dryly. "I would wager that whatever is tattled from gentlemen to carriage will be to your advantage. At any rate, if the news chances to reach him, your father should be pleased. I doubt a father would chastise you for having your life saved."

Emma could see the truth of this. She attempted a serene smile in the vague direction of the cluster of carriages, and murmured, "I believe we shall prevail."

He waited as the viscount and Gussie led the way from the racecourse, then fell in behind them. The Stanwell carriage brought up the rear of the little cavalcade.

Emma couldn't resist a backward glance to where Claude sat opposite the earl and his countess. The landau was at an angle to the cabriolet so she just caught his profile. In spite of his initial pout, he looked to relish being in the earl's crested carriage. He obviously liked the impressive array.

And her father's money could buy a fair amount of such splendor. Indeed, she would do well to keep an eye on him. Did Claude possibly fear rivalry from Mr. Herbert in spite of the fact she had many times made it clear she would never marry her cousin? What an impossible situation!

She shifted around to stare ahead, thinking furiously. From the few words Mr. Herbert had uttered regarding her cousin Claude, Emma gathered he was not to be trusted. Not that she had trusted him in the past at all. She wrenched her mind from her cousin to the matters at hand.

"So that is why I am to ride home with you? I imagine I ought to look suitably thrilled?" Emma forced a smile.

"As to that, I suppose a properly adoring look would help the cause along." He tossed her a casual glance that sent a quiver through her that had nothing to do with the aches from her tumble.

His gray eyes glittered with what she interpreted as scorn and succeeded in completely silencing her for a time.

Not so Mr. Herbert. "Are you surprised that your pretty friend was taken up by my cousin Rawlinson? I must say, he seems rather taken with her. Is he given to flirting?"

Emma considered the matter a little, then said, "I do not think he is. At least," she amended, "I have never heard anything to that effect. Gussie is the dearest girl. I trust Rawlinson will behave with propriety. I'd not like to see her heart wounded."

"Somehow I doubt that will happen. She appears to be prudent—proper and yet not prim." A note of admiration rang in his voice.

Stung by the implication that Mr. Herbert might consider Emma to be improper and too free in her manner, she subsided, trying to think of a good retort. Nothing came to mind.

"My great-aunt and uncle seem to feel you are worth

safeguarding," he added, clearly believing the opposite. "Lady Stanwell suggested we plan a number of excursions to nearby spots of interest. Evidently if several of us are seen out and about it will be plain to one and all that we are one jolly group and accepted by the earl. We wouldn't want it put about that you hold me in aversion merely because I tumbled you in the grass, now would we? Besides, we shall go to places where there aren't likely to be any tipsy gentlemen. You need have no fear on that score." Again his voice brimmed with irony.

She ignored his reference to the somewhat foxed man who pushed her onto the racecourse. And why did she have the feeling that underneath Mr. Herbert's reserve he was laughing at her? She found it difficult to believe he was the son of a rector. He did not appear to be solemn and certainly wasn't the sort to spout scripture at the drop of a hat. She had encountered one of that kind.

"You mean like Avebury, and the Kennet and Avon canal, possibly Stonehenge?" She utterly ignored the bit about holding him in aversion. Of course she didn't, but on the other hand she thought it sensible to avoid saying anything else. Even if his "tumbling" her in the grass had forced an early departure from the races, created gossip, and stirred strange feelings deep inside her, she thought it best to remain silent.

"I suggested a shopping expedition to Bath. If we are all seen as a cheerful party in Bath, who can quibble?"

"Bath," Emma uttered reverently. "Oh, I hope we can go there. I can think of any number of things I should like to purchase." She began to make a mental list.

"Like ordering a pelisse of the latest style, new bonnets, and gloves, I suppose." He chuckled, and Emma instantly felt more in charity with him.

"To be sure. Music and books as well."

"I know you play the harp, but I had not thought you a reader, Miss Lawrence. Do not tell me you are a bluestocking. I'd not believe it."

"I daresay you don't think me much of anything, Mr. Herbert," she retorted, somehow hurt by the notion that Mr. Herbert might not hold her in the slightest esteem.

Adam glanced at the spirited young woman at his side. He doubted she would believe what he thought of her if he told her.

When the little cavalcade rolled into Marlborough it was midafternoon.

The earl called a halt at the Castle Inn again, but this time to enjoy a meal. Adam suspected Emma Lawrence thought it had been a long day. It seemed so to him. He figured that by the time they consumed a meal it would be late.

The group who gathered in a private parlor of the inn was a gay lot. Naturally, Claude indicated his displeasure at being odd man out, treating the other young people with more than his customary disdain. Riding in the earl's carriage must have gone to his head.

How he thought they might pull a suitable lady from thin air was beyond Adam. Rawlinson, Gussie Dunlop, and Emma Lawrence were agreeable company. Claude Polkinghorne could jolly well sulk. He had been that way at Cambridge, Adam recalled. He'd always wanted to have his way.

The earl had ordered with a lavish hand. Shortly the large table was spread with a nice selection of viands.

Emma was particularly pleased to see mushroom fritters, one of her favorite foods. Gussie teased her about it.

"One of these days you will turn into a mushroom,

Emma." Gussie giggled softly before responding to something said to her by Lord Rawlinson.

"I shall spring up overnight!" Emma joked.

She watched the pair, who appeared to take simple pleasure in the meal. They chatted and laughed as though they had known each other for years. It was so unlike the Rawlinson she remembered that she couldn't have said a word for anything. Her memory of Rawlinson was of someone terribly puffed up with himself, dressing in the very latest styles, repeating the current gossip from London. He had been her ultimate idea of a dandy. She avoided Stanwell Hall on the rare occasions he came to visit. Consequently, she didn't know him well. It didn't matter. She truly had not wished to know him better. This present side of him was most illuminating. She wondered why he was here.

"What brings you to the country, Rawlinson?" she inquired, giving voice to her thoughts.

"London is terribly thin of acceptable company this time of year. Rather than visit friends, I decided to come home. It has been an age since I was last here. But I fully intend to remain for a time—if my grandparents will allow." He looked to the earl and countess.

"I am sure you are welcome to remain as long as you please. You will no doubt wish to become better acquainted with your cousin Adam." The countess nodded from one gentleman to the other in a regal manner.

That Rawlinson subsequently looked at Gussie with more than a little appreciation was not lost on Adam.

He studied the fellow across from him. He wasn't precisely a dandy, but he certainly had elegant taste in waistcoats, not to mention a clever way with a cravat. If not mistaken, he had tied the mathematical cravat style today and Adam longed to perfect it. Perhaps if the viscount was still here when they made the excursion to

Bath he might be willing to offer a word of advice on a waistcoat. Adam had no intention of attempting to be fashionable, but he'd like to cut a modest dash. He should be able to obtain a decent waistcoat for around a pound or so.

The earl declared that after such a meal, they had best walk around for a little before settling in the carriages again. The remainder of the drive would take perhaps an hour and a half.

Adam assisted Miss Lawrence from her chair, then ushered her from the private parlor. He had been raised with five sisters and thought he had a fair notion of what Miss Lawrence was thinking.

It had been a difficult day for her. No young woman likes to be the object of ridicule or gossip. He would wager that while she was something of a madcap, she never intentionally went beyond the bounds of what was truly proper.

Once they all were outside, strolling around on the grounds of the inn, Adam placed her hand on his arm, thus keeping her close to his side.

Her gaze was questioning, but she didn't pull away.

"I want no accidents here." He was intrigued to see that she cast a look at her cousin Claude. Adam was of a like mind—he didn't trust Polkinghorne either.

"I have the oddest feeling that what happened at the racecourse was no accident." She prudently kept her voice low so her words could not be overheard.

"That has occurred to me as well. Somehow seeing Polkinghorne chatting with a tipsy chap seemed quite out of line. Not his style at all, if you know what I mean."

"I agree. However, there is nothing of which he might be accused at this point. Merely talking to someone does not convict him of dire desires on my inheritance."

"I hope we can avoid taking him along on these excursions Stanwell proposed." Adam doubted they might avoid the chap.

"Be careful of what you say in that regard, then," she advised. "I believe they tolerate Claude because he is my cousin and, as well, he is a neighbor. If he doesn't know where and when we go, we ought to have nothing to worry about."

Adam gave Claude a troubled look. He hoped it was that simple.

At that moment Gussie summoned them to join in an attempt at quoits.

Adam proved adept at the game. Emma did far better than he expected, given her reluctance to throw the quoit at the hob. The second of her quoits she sent sailing the distance to the far hob dug nicely into the dirt, giving her a ringer.

"Well done!" he exclaimed, pleased when he saw the pretty color flood her cheeks.

"Living in the country has its uses. When we get together we have simple pleasures, of which quoits is one."

Adam picked up his two quoits as well as hers, joining her near where the others stood, laughing and joking about the ability or lack thereof to send that flattish iron ring sailing the nineteen feet to the other hob.

It wasn't long before the earl's groom approached with the news that it was time to depart.

Strolling to where the carriages now awaited them, Adam studied the signs where the roads intersected. "You said something about seeing Avebury. I see a sign pointing that way. So we would come here, then go west. Is that right?"

"I believe there is another road you might take, but this is the better one, I think. And Silbury Hill is close to Avebury. There is naught but an enormous mound of dirt at Silbury, but it is rather awesome to think of people piling up so much dirt in one place. No one has the slightest idea as to why or what it means."

Adam assisted her into the cabriolet, then joined her. "I can see I am to be educated on this trip."

"How long do you plan to stay?" Emma ventured. It wasn't precisely the most civil question, she supposed. However, she did want to know. Why was another matter altogether.

"I wonder if we could combine seeing those with our expedition to Bath?" He didn't reply to her query, rather he negotiated their way through a throng of coaches, wagons, and carriages making their way in and out of Marlborough. At last, clear of other vehicles, they headed south toward Peetbridge and Stanwell Hall.

"It would involve several days of traveling and staying in inns, I should imagine. Not that it couldn't be done, mind you." She gave him a puzzled look.

"I will discuss it with my great-uncle. He may have some suggestions." Adam again followed Rawlinson, with the earl's carriage right behind them. No one had suggested that anyone change places, which Adam found intriguing. It would seem that the countess had no objection to his interest in Miss Lawrence. He imagined that a woman of her years would be able to see in a moment that such an interest on his part existed. In spite of her somewhat hoydenish ways, Adam found Emma captivating.

They again changed horses at the inn near Pewsey. Adam was glad to have his own horse again. Jigg looked well rested and more than ready to trot on to Stanwell Hall.

"Stonehenge is south of us. If you just kept going on this road you would eventually reach the turn that would take you to that site. I have never been there, but I have heard it is most impressive." She sounded rather wistful.

"Then we should make a point of going. I want to see all that I can while here." The thought of leaving this lovely area brought a pang of sadness. Though Kent possessed its share of beauty, this was beautiful country. There was something very appealing in the rolling downs, so green and lush. They held a vastness he liked. The chance he would be able to find a church in need of a vicar in this area would be highly unlikely.

"What do you plan to do when you return to your home?"

She was an inquisitive miss, for certain. What could he tell her? That he intended to apply for a position as an assistant to a land manager? Or a steward's aide? There was not a thing wrong with either position, but he wondered what Miss Lawrence of Brook Court would say to that?

"I have nothing definite in mind at this time. I should like to have something to do with land, caring for it or managing it." That was sufficiently vague.

"So you do not intend to follow your father into the church?" She stared at him, curiosity clear.

"No." He didn't go into the explanation he could have offered—that few openings existed and, in addition, he did not feel a call to the ministry. She asked no more questions, and he put aside his dreams.

By the time they reached Stanwell Hall, everyone was tired, thirsty, and a little hungry.

The countess invited them all to come into the house. Once inside, Adam studied Claude. He remembered that Mr. Lawrence had gone to Salisbury and wasn't due home until tomorrow. He met the countess's gaze and strolled over to join her.

"Dear ma'am, I wonder if perhaps Miss Lawrence ought to remain here for the night? Her father is not yet home, and from hints she has given, I sense that Polkinghorne has intimidated the servants to obey him. Might it not be wise if she was out of his reach?" From where he watched, it was clear to him that Claude had a predatory gleam in his eyes when he looked at Emma Lawrence.

"Wise, indeed. The housekeeper might be remarkable in that the house is always just so. However, I doubt she would protect Emma from the advances of a man known to be preferred by Mr. Lawrence. Trust me to see to it."

Shortly, the countess summoned Emma to her side.

"My dear, I wish you to remain here for the night. With your father gone, it will be a bit lonely for you to return to an empty house. I will have Nancy find you a night robe and send one of the footmen to inform Mrs. Turner so she won't be concerned when you fail to return home. We can enjoy a pleasant visit in the morning and discuss some plans."

That there were numerous servants at Brook Court was ignored. As far as agreeable company, Emma would be alone.

Emma caught the inflection in Countess Stanwell's voice at once. The countess had glanced at Claude as she spoke, although she hadn't said anything specific in regards to him. Coming so soon after the incident at the racecourse, Emma agreed it would be wise.

"What about Gussie?" Emma wondered aloud. "I think we ought to include her on any plans."

The countess took another look at her grandson where he sat by Gussie, chatting with more enthusiasm than she had seen heretofore. "Hmm, I see what you mean. I shall order a room prepared for her as well. The footman can go to both houses."

When informed of the treat, Gussie bloomed with a sweet blush, a demure sweep of her lashes covering her confusion.

Not invited to stay, Claude took reluctant leave of the group. He offered to give Emma a ride home and seemed most displeased when informed that the countess wished her to stay overnight.

"Dash it all, Emma, your father thinks you are at home. There is no need for you to stay here."

"Nonsense!" she snapped back. Emma decided that from now on when her father took an overnight trip she would either stay with Gussie or beg the countess to help.

Once Claude left, the entire group seemed to relax into a pleasant informality.

Precedence was ignored when they went in to enjoy the late supper laid out for them.

Emma's heart took an odd little leap when Adam Herbert placed her hand on his arm. It was strange, Gussie seemed to behave with the most natural air when the viscount escorted her. Yet Emma felt tongue-tied and her knees were shaking. She must have been out in the sun too long.

Yet she could not ignore the admiration in Mr. Herbert's eyes. It seemed he found her to his liking after all. She tried to be calm, but inwardly her heart was in turmoil. Riding beside him in the cabriolet was one thing, for they were out where they could be seen by everyone. Going in to supper on his arm seemed more intimate, somehow.

Later when she thought about it, she couldn't remember a morsel she ate. She had listened to the countess and the earl offer ideas for their amusement. When Bath was suggested, Emma finally found her voice.

"I should like that above all things, ma'am."

"We shall all go. Except for Claude, of course. I do not see why he should be included. It makes our numbers uneven. Tomorrow we will make more definite plans. I suppose you must await your father's approval?" she said to Emma.

"True." Emma wondered if her loquacious father would mention the excursions to Claude. The two of them were as thick as thieves.

She would have to hope for the best.

Chapter Seven

It seemed strange to wake in a room not her own. Looking about her, Emma thought the Rose Room to be all a young lady could desire. A comfortable walnut four-post bed sat against the inner wall, so she could look out into the treetops, now a rich deep green in late summer. The morning sun streamed in through the opened rose-print chintz draperies. She was at Stanwell Hall, in a room she loved.

Turning her head, she saw the small chintz-covered chair before a pretty dressing table, waiting for her to use it. To one side of the room stood an impressive walnut chest and near it a wardrobe of massive proportions, also walnut, and most likely empty but for the dress Mrs. Turner had sent over.

When she left the bed her feet sank into the rich Wilton carpet with a rose design. Her room at home was pretty, but this room was splendid. Nancy ably helped her into her dress. With her hair neatly arranged, the simple sarcenet dress required nothing more than a light shawl over her shoulders. First thanking the maid, she left her room to break her fast.

She sauntered down the stairs in the quiet house, wondering what she would feel when she saw Adam Herbert again. He created such conflicting sensations within her. Part of her thought him quite handsome.

His thick auburn hair was always neatly groomed and picked up golden glints from the sun. And his gray eyes twinkled when he smiled down at her, which seemed often. Except, of course, when he was furious with her over some little thing she had done—such as the incident at the racecourse.

Part of her still trembled when she thought of the contretemps at the racecourse. She vividly recalled the feel of his muscular body against hers. He had offered protection and strength.

She couldn't understand why her knees were so unsteady when she met that gray gaze or why her stomach felt as though she was rapidly driving up and down hills in a runaway chaise whenever he was close to her or took her hand. She had never experienced anything like it in her life, and she wasn't sure she liked it.

Certainly her cousin, the dastardly Claude, had no effect on her other than complete distaste.

When Emma entered the breakfast room she discovered that Mr. Herbert and Rawlinson were there before her, tucking into a hearty meal. Her heart did a couple of flip-flops, then settled down while she went about the mundane task of selecting food.

Mr. Herbert hastily rose to assist Emma to a chair after she had chosen her morning meal from the sideboard. She ate lightly, toast and preserves, a bit of fruit and ham.

"You are up betimes this morning," she said to Rawlinson.

"We have a bit of planning to do if we are to make that trip to Bath. Grandfather wants me to send a message to the Castle Inn regarding rooms for us. Seems there is a small fair in town he thought we might enjoy."

Emma said nothing to this, but a flicker of excitement darted through her. Even country fairs were a novelty for her.

"And he agreed that we might stop at Beckhampton Inn to spend some time seeing Avebury and Silbury Hill. I'll send on to book rooms for us there." He paused as though to consider what was next to decide. "Grandmother is of a mind to stay at the White Hart Inn while in Bath, although Grandfather insists that York House is more to his liking. Do you have an opinion?"

"Goodness," Emma replied, "I scarce know what to say on the matter, not having been there since I was a child."

She listened silently while the two men discussed the possibilities for their grand excursion. It was like a dream. Things she had longed to do, places she wanted to see, were all coming about because of Adam Herbert. She must think kindly of him if only for that reason.

Shortly after they finished eating, it was decided that both Rawlinson and Mr. Herbert would accompany Emma to her home to persuade her father to allow her to join the group headed for Bath and all the interesting places in between.

She must have looked dubious, for as they left the breakfast room Mr. Herbert queried her, "Surely your father would not deny you this treat?"

"Emma's father is not the doting sort," Rawlinson dryly commented. "It is anyone's guess what he will say."

They left Stanwell Hall shortly after noon, hoping to find that Mr. Lawrence had returned by that time. They were in luck. He came into view as they wound around to the stable block. He stopped in his tracks to study the trio.

"What's this, Emma? Mrs. Turner tells me you remained at Stanwell last night." He walked over to meet the carriage as the viscount brought the team to a halt.

"I went to the races north of Marlborough yesterday, and the countess insisted I remain overnight rather than go home in the dark after we had a supper," Emma replied sedately. "She was concerned for my safety, Papa."

She left the carriage to join her father. Once at his side, she tugged on his sleeve. "You know Viscount Rawlinson. I should like to make the Stanwells' great-nephew known to you."

She kept an eye on her father as she made the proper introductions. He should be pleased she had such a distinguished escort. He gave no indication of it one way or the other, and merely gestured for them to join him in the house.

The butler ushered them into the entry hall with an obsequious bow. He murmured something about waiting mail, and then left to fetch the beverages he knew would be wanted.

The four strolled into the small drawing room just off the entry. Done in shades of blue and white, the room looked comfortable and well used. Not that it was shabby by any means, but it was of an older style and just as Mrs. Lawrence had left it years ago when she died. Nothing had been altered.

"Papa, the countess has a request of you," Emma began as they paused in the center of the room. Then, at a significant look from the viscount, she became silent. Perhaps it would be better were he to ask.

"Indeed, sir, my grandparents are planning a little

jaunt to Bath with stops along the way to show their great-nephew a bit of the country. They wish Emma to join the party. We intend to ask Miss Dunlop as well. There will be six of us, plus maids and grooms. The girls will be well chaperoned."

"The great-nephew, eh?" Mr. Lawrence said with a curious look at the stranger. "From down in Kent, I understand? Father is a rector there?"

"Yes, sir," Mr. Herbert replied pleasantly.

"Gussie as well? But not Claude?" Mr. Lawrence frowned.

"No, Papa. I believe it would be too many." Emma had no idea what else to offer as an excuse. She could only hope that her father would not make an issue of the matter. Claude might be her heir, but it didn't mean he had to be invited.

Her father gave her a keen look, quite as though he suspected the truth and did not like it.

"Please, Papa. I have nearly all my quarterly allowance left to spend in Bath. I should dearly like to have a new bonnet, and perhaps some other things as well."

"Maybe Emma has made too many trips to Bath?" The viscount's bantering voice intruded into her argument.

She whirled to face Rawlinson, ready to scold.

He gave her the faintest shake of his head.

Mr. Lawrence looked a trifle abashed. "As to that, I disremember when Emma has gone to Bath. She stays around home for the most part. Claude could take her, I suppose."

"Papa, I would never go anywhere with cousin Claude. *Never.* I would truly enjoy the trip with the Stanwells. The countess is the dearest lady and most motherly."

As Emma suspected, her father bristled at the thought of her lack of a mother. "Well . . ."

"Please, dear Papa."

"Very well. I shall ride over to discuss the matter with the earl. But if I know the countess, she has her plans all made and they include you no matter what I say on it."

"Jolly good, sir. We will continue on to the Dunlops in that event. Do you come with us, Emma?" the viscount asked.

"I had best pack my things. Let me know the hour we are to leave." She took a step toward the door, then paused. "Unless the countess wishes me to stay overnight in the event of an early departure?"

"I will send a message," the viscount promised.

She saw them out, then hurried up to her room. The less time she spent with her father, the less chance there was that he would change his mind.

Mrs. Dunlop agreed at once to the proposed excursion. "Augusta and Emma have always been close. I am sure they will both enjoy the experience." She gave her pretty redheaded daughter a fond look.

Gussie seemed happy enough to float all the way to Stanwell Hall. That her eyes often strayed to the fine figure of the viscount wasn't missed by Adam or her mother. If Viscount Rawlinson seemed less than formal toward Augusta Dunlop it was not the least noteworthy or objectionable.

Since Hanover, Mr. Dunlop, and his entourage had returned, the young men asked to see the famous horse. Gussie displayed the impressive gold plate that Hanover had won, then escorted the guests to the stable block.

As soon as they were away from the house and before they reached the stables, Gussie turned to Rawlinson. "Is Emma truly being allowed to go with us? I can scarce believe her father will permit it. And Claude Polkinghorne not one of the party? Amazing!" Her voice was tinged with irony.

The viscount and Adam exchanged looks, but merely affirmed that Emma would be one of the party going to Bath.

Adam admired Hanover while Rawlinson spoke to Mr. Dunlop. He listened to the proposal with a smile. "It's fine with me. The countess is one for propriety. But I'll not allow her to stand my girl's expenses. We are well able to afford a trip like this. And, my dear Gussie, you shall have a tidy sum to waste on a new bonnet and the fal-lals you girls like so much." He smiled wryly at her glowing face when she heard his promise.

So it was that the girls came to spend the night at Stanwell Hall, prepared to leave early in the morning.

The earl demanded nicely that Emma play a few of his favorite pieces on the harp following dinner.

"Didn't have that tuned to gather dust. I'll hear some music, my girl." He listened with obvious enjoyment, which made it just as agreeable for Emma.

She observed that Mr. Herbert appeared to enjoy the harp music as well. He applauded heartily when she concluded.

They all went up to bed early that evening. Mr. Herbert and Rawlinson bowed over the girls' hands with gentlemanlike manners. Emma thought she caught a wicked gleam in the eyes of each gentleman. She was sufficiently wise to make no comment on that!

Gussie and Emma floated down the hall to the bedroom. "Thank heavens Claude is excluded," Emma whispered to her friend.

"Indeed, he has a way of spoiling things. What a pity your father is so blind to his faults."

Emma didn't argue with that sentiment. She had thought the same any number of times.

They entered the bedroom, thankful for the small coal fire burning in the grate. It might be summer, but this year it had not been a warm one—at least so far. Some years, autumn turned out to be the best season of the year.

"I not only have my allowance, but Papa gave me a fine number of pounds over," Emma said, still amazed at this. "I'm glad the earl has an outrider as well as a well-armed coachman. I'd not want to have my precious money stolen!" She tucked some of her funds in her reticule, the remainder in her valise.

She surveyed her old reticule with a rueful face. "One thing I shall purchase is a new reticule. This one is sadly lacking, I fear."

Gussie giggled, replying, "Papa was most handsome in my spending money, too. We shall have a wonderful time in Bath."

"And all points in between. Oh, Gussie, do you think the trip will be auspicious? I have seen the way Rawlinson looks at you. And you return that look. It would be a marvelous thing were he to be truly taken with you."

Gussie blushed, cautioning her dearest friend, "It is improbable. Why, he could choose anyone. Why would he look twice at a redheaded country girl like me? I think you had best go to sleep. Morning will come before you know it."

Since they had decided to share the rose bedroom, Emma smiled and rolled over in the vast bed. Gussie blew out the candle and continued to speculate for at least thirty minutes longer on the delights in store for them in the coming days.

It seemed that Emma had just closed her eyes when the maid, Nancy, entered to wake them.

The girls eagerly dressed in their best traveling costumes. Gussie wore a pomona-green kerseymere pelisse over a delicate cream India muslin gown trimmed with pomona-green riband.

Emma thought her rich blue sarcenet pelisse over her equally nice blue-sprigged muslin a fine contrast to Gussie. That the deep blue reflected the blue of her eyes was an added delight. Neither garment was new nor of the latest style. However, they flattered her and were comfortable and there was much to be said for such. When one had to rely on a rural seamstress one could not be too particular.

Perhaps she might indulge in more shopping. She had saved a fair sum from her previous quarter's allowance—what was there to spend on in the country? She had not confided such to Gussie, but if they had the time, Emma wanted to see if she could find a new garment. Surely some mantua-maker might have a dress or pelisse that would fit her and look well?

Following a light meal, the group set forth toward Marlborough with high spirits.

Adam and Rawlinson drove in his cabriolet, while the girls joined the earl and countess in the traveling carriage. As they approached the town it soon became evident that a smallish fair was in progress. The broad street was filled with animals, people, and those peripatetic entertainers who traveled from one fair to another to amuse people and thus earn their bread.

Emma gave a small bounce of excitement. Papa had never permitted her to attend one of these little country fairs, much less one of the larger ones, such as a mop fair where he went to engage new workers. She felt like a bird released from a cage.

Mr. Herbert gallantly assisted the countess and Emma from the carriage. The viscount took Gussie's hand, then tucked her hand next to his side, with the comment, "I do not wish you to get lost, my dear."

The earl, handed down by a groom, took a narrow perusal of the couple and turned to his wife. "Sits the wind in that quarter, does it?" he murmured.

"We shall see, my dear." She gave a dismissing wave of her hand to Mr. Herbert and Emma, sending them off in the same direction that Gussie and Rawlinson had gone.

Adam took a page from his cousin and gathered Miss Lawrence close to his side. He was rewarded with a glowing look.

"I shall try hard not to disgrace you today, Mr. Herbert."

"Since we are to be traveling together for some days, I wonder if it might be permissible for us to be less formal. I noticed that Rawlinson calls your friend Gussie. Might I use your lovely name . . . Emma?" He guided her around a flock of sheep, past a team of horses, and straight to a fairing booth.

"For bringing me to the fairing booth, you may call me anything you please. I have never had something like this." Her face wore an eager expression as she examined the trifles sold to fair-goers. There were pretty glass beads and broaches in many colors, whistles, tiny china and pottery animals and sentimental figures. Off to one side were wooden toys. Emma's hand strayed to a china heart.

"Allow me . . . Emma?" Adam gently removed the little heart, noting the dainty flowers painted on the top.

"Forget-me-nots. How appropriate." He paid for the heart, handing the charming trifle to the bubbling young woman at his side.

"Thank you." She seemed a bit embarrassed at accepting the china heart, little though it might be.

"'Tis nothing. Now," Adam pointed to the next booth where an old lady was doing a brisk business in selling ginger nuts, "I believe we must try a few of these." As he paid for the treats he wondered how far the money advanced to him by his father would extend. He intended to pay for his room and he dearly wanted to buy a new waistcoat if such was obtainable ready-made in Bath. Well, he wouldn't be extravagant. Surely a few little treats for Miss Lawrence would be permissible.

They wandered along the booths crammed cheek by jowl on the main street. It was a good thing the street was so broad. There was still ample room for the carriages that dashed through Marlborough going east and west.

A table piled high with tea-caddies vied with another loaded with cheeses. A Punch and Judy show delighted youngsters.

"There is a fortune teller's tent. I should like to see what she foresees for me. And . . . my good sir, I shan't allow you to pay my nonsense. I insist. I have ample funds for all I want, and I suspect you do not quite approve of fortune-telling." She was far too tactful to suggest he might have limited funds.

"You have the right of it, although I suppose they are harmless enough." He paused to give the gaudy tent a dubious perusal. "If you are determined, I'll wait here for you."

Emma laughed and went to open the flap of the tent. As she did, something caught her eye. Could that have been Claude she just spotted? He had a coat exactly that color, and the man was his height. Alarmed, she paused a moment, then decided she must have been seeing things. She slipped into the tent, a rising tingle of excitement surging through her.

Coin in hand, she perched on the edge of the wooden stool, waiting. The scarves and veils made it hard to see precisely how old the gypsy was. When she spoke her voice cracked and her hands were darkly veined and somewhat withered.

"The silver, please, missy."

Emma hesitantly extended her hand with the coin. The dryness of the gypsy's voice was not unexpected. The subtle fragrance of incense haunted the table where she sat. Emma knew a sudden desire to flee and forget the coin. An eerie feeling pervaded the tent.

"You want to know the future, eh?" The crone studied the slim hand in hers. She frowned and Emma wondered if that was for effect.

"You shall find your heart's desire, but not easily. There is one who would keep you from happiness. Beware of him."

Claude, Emma decided. "But I will find happiness?"

"Indeed, if you do not muddle matters up, you will. You will have a fine home and much wealth. I foresee four children."

A hint of a smile lurked at the corner of Emma's mouth. "Do any of them perchance have auburn hair?"

The gypsy gazed at Emma with what appeared to be a sparkle in her dark eyes. "It is possible."

Laughing at the images in her mind, Emma left the tent, relieved to be out in the sunshine if the truth be known. There had been an odd atmosphere in the tent, one she could not like.

"And what did you learn, fair lady?" Mr. Herbert teased. "Shall you marry a wealthy man and have a fine family?"

"How perceptive you are. She promised me wealth and a fine home—if I don't muddle things up. I wonder how or why I would do that?" Emma said nothing about four children who possibly might have auburn hair.

The countess and Gussie joined them and demanded to know what the fortune-teller had predicted for Emma. When she revealed the danger of one who would keep her from knowing happiness, Gussie sniffed.

"If that isn't Claude I don't know who it would be."

"Indeed, I meet so many people." Emma couldn't keep the faint bitterness from her voice. What was the point of being a fine heiress if the only man she ever saw was Claude? She intended to make the most of this excursion. She was aware there might be problems with Mr. Herbert—Adam. He was surprisingly lordly in his behavior. One might think he was related to the peerage. Then she recalled he was. A great-nephew was not close, but close enough. Certainly he was closer than Claude was!

"And did she promise you would wed a tall, dark, and handsome gentleman?" the countess cried laughingly.

"Well, that would be telling," Emma retorted with a grin. "However, I am to marry well and have a fine house. How I am to meet this mysterious gentleman is beyond me, since Papa keeps me home most of the time. You do not know, dear ma'am, how happy I am to be on this jaunt of yours. I am grateful to Mr. Herbert for visiting so that we may have such a splendid treat!"

They all smiled, turning to retrace their steps in the direction of the Castle Inn.

Suddenly Gussie said, "I vow I saw Claude a moment ago. Do you believe he might attend the fair?"

"I can't imagine why. His father never allows him to make any purchases for the estate. Yet I thought I glimpsed him as well," Emma replied, a concerned note in her voice.

"Absurd, of course" Gussie murmured.

They entered the inn, going promptly to the private dining parlor reserved for their use. The earl was waiting for them, at ease in a comfortable chair by the window that overlooked the garden in the back of the inn.

"I suppose Emma found the fortune-teller's tent?"

Gussie glanced at her friend, then ventured to say, "She did and was promised a fine home and wealth. How many children?"

"Gussie, I declare, you are impossible. I shan't tell you how many children she said, for it likely is nonsense."

Gussie made no comment on the slight blush that spread across Emma's cheeks. Emma could feel the heat and only hoped that Mr. Herbert would make nothing of it.

They spent the rest of the afternoon wandering along the street, mostly just looking at the various attractions. When dusk approached, the earl shepherded them all back to the Castle Inn for supper.

"It gets a bit rowdy come evening," was his explanation.

Later when they were all cozy in their rooms, Gussie, who shared a room with Emma, studied her old friend. "Emma, I hope you are not getting a *tendré* for Mr. Herbert. You know full well that your father would never permit you to marry him."

Emma sank down on the edge of her bed with a fervent sigh. Fingering the little china heart, she said, "How true. But Gussie," she said softly, "I shall do what I can to make my dreams come true." That her dreams centered around a man she had reason to believe disliked her was but a minor problem.

•

Chapter Eight

"Emma, I hope you are not getting a *tendré* for Mr. Herbert. You know full well that your father would never permit you to marry him." The voice was somewhat muffled but could be made out by those listening in the quiet of the evening.

"That was Gussie," Rawlinson said unnecessarily. The young gentlemen in the adjacent room heard with dismay the words spoken rather loudly by Emma's dear friend.

"I can't make out a reply—if there was one," Adam said with a rueful grimace. "Well, it does put me in my place." He walked to the window to stare with unseeing eyes at the scene below where the traders were packing up for the day. "Not that I believe there would be a chance her father would look favorably on my suit—in the event I had one, that is. Which I do not."

Rawlinson straddled a wooden chair, leaning his chin on the top of it while considering what had been overheard. "But it does reveal that Gussie believes Emma Lawrence has a decided partiality for you. I doubt Gussie would say anything without reason," he pointed out in fairness.

"She assumes a great deal. As the son of a minister I am an unlikely candidate for marriage to anyone, let alone someone as lovely and gifted as Miss Lawrence."

There was no hint of bitterness in Adam's voice. He had accepted his lot and saw no way to change matters. He wasn't given to gambling, and that was a popular way to obtain funds, if you were lucky.

"She is that," Rawlinson mused. "No money, eh?" he asked, although suspecting it was the truth. Few rectors were wealthy, even in a prosperous parish. "No private income?"

"A little, but with six children in the family it has been spread rather thin." Adam grimaced ruefully.

"I met your sister Penelope in London, you know. The last I heard she was to marry Lord Latimer. That hasn't altered?"

"No, they are wed. My sister Nympha is an heiress, married to Lord Nicholas Stanhope. My sister Tabitha is wed to Lord Latham—who has a fine estate. And Drusilla is to marry the Marquess of Brentford before long. Still, I can't and won't batten onto them. What decent man would?" Adam gave his cousin a defiant stare.

"More than you know, old chap. I'd be surprised if they didn't do something for you, though. Family ties, and all that." Rawlinson studied Adam with a frowning gaze. "Perhaps if each . . ."

"It is a moot point—at least nothing has been said. The most I would ask is a kind word when I seek a position."

"A position!" Rawlinson sat up and stared at Adam in obvious dismay. "Oh, I say now!"

"What I want most of all is to manage land. I thought to train under a really good man, then proceed on my own. Or do you think I am mad?"

"Your Latin would come in handy when ordering plants," Rawlinson said dryly, subsiding on the chair again.

Adam nodded. "Well, little point in pondering on it now. Unless you happen to know of someone looking for an assistant steward?" Adam walked to stand by the fireplace where a fitful fire smoldered in the grate. He stared into the glowing coals.

"Discuss it with my grandfather. He'll know. You might even be able to apprentice under his steward." Rawlinson rose from the chair, and when Hilton, his valet, entered the room, began to prepare for bed. Adam, without a valet, did the same, dropping his boots while ruing their lack of shine.

They abandoned the subject. When Hilton departed with both pairs of boots, following a signal from his master, the men retired. The room was spacious, with two narrow beds of considerable comfort for them.

Long after the candles had been snuffed out, Adam considered his dilemma. Emma Lawrence might be delightful, but he had best forget about her . . . at least after this excursion was over. He consoled himself that she was a headstrong lass and would likely be troublesome to handle. Not that he truly believed anyone could "handle" a woman of her mettle. It would take cleverness to make her believe your way was hers.

He wasn't the man for the job—not that it didn't have its challenge. And Adam had always enjoyed a challenge.

In the adjacent bedchamber Gussie slept soundly while poor Emma tossed and turned fitfully most of the night. Consequently, when the maid came to wake the girls, she was not in the best humor.

"You look in the dismals, dearest. I would say offhand that you did not sleep well. I do hope it wasn't what I said before we climbed into bed?" Gussie inquired anxiously.

"Well, it did give me pause. You see, Gussie, it made me think. You know I am determined *not* to marry Claude."

"I should hope not," Gussie muttered.

"I must wonder how in the world I am to meet a gentleman who not only pleases me but will prove acceptable to Papa as well. I expect it would have to be someone with good prospects. Even if Claude doesn't have a cent to spare, that makes little difference to *his* qualification. Since I never go anywhere—other than to Stanwell Hall or your house, and a few others—where could I meet any eligible gentlemen?"

Emma glowered at her friend. It was so frustrating. Her own father was determined to have his way even if his only child would be made dreadfully unhappy as a result of his resolve to have the money remain in the family. Spinsterhood loomed on the horizon as an attractive alternative to Claude.

"You do not," Gussie agreed. "I have seen a few decent sorts at the Salisbury assembly. What a pity your father wouldn't let you go with me. But *that* might lead you away from Claude." Gussie made a face. "Still, meeting someone eligible while in Salisbury isn't truly helpful. The distance is an obstacle. On the other hand you . . ."

"I have a fortune large enough to tempt any man. I wonder if Mr. Herbert has been told about it?" Emma paused while slipping on her dress, giving Gussie an inquiring glance.

Gussie gave her an arrested look. "Somehow I doubt it would matter to him one way or the other. He strikes me as a man of integrity, not the sort to be a fortune hunter."

"I agree. You met the viscount at Stanwell," Emma reminded. "I have met no one until Mr. Herbert arrived.

Rawlinson doesn't count—we brangle over everything. It is a pity Mr. Herbert is ineligible. He is rather handsome." Emma brushed down her attractive traveling dress before adding, "There is now a problem in attracting anyone locally. I fear that word of the scandalous happening at the racecourse has spread. I didn't mention it last night, but the number of raised brows and whispered comments I observed yesterday forced me to draw that conclusion. If people think I am outrageous, how will I *ever* attract anyone? Only a desperate man would apply!"

"Well, you might deliberately cultivate that reputation, I guess," Gussie said jokingly. When she caught sight of the thoughtful expression on her friend's face she added in a horrified manner, "I didn't mean that, Emma. It was merely said in jest."

"You don't think I ought to actually be a madcap? That I ought to be as outrageous as people believe I am?"

"Please consider, my dear. You do not wish to remain at Brook Court, do you? You do not want to be compelled to wed Claude, I know. But would your father accept any other?"

"Claude is such a nodcock he'd not marry someone with a scandalous reputation, not even for the money."

Gussie gave her friend a dubious look. "I wouldn't be too sure of that were I you." She finished doing up the back of Emma's dress.

Emma jammed on her bonnet before grabbing her gloves and reticule. "Oh, rubbish."

With that pungent observation, the girls hurried down to the private parlor where the others had assembled. The viscount immediately took Gussie in hand. Emma quickly joined the countess, pouring tea for those who wished and coffee for the earl. Rawlinson had a mug of home-brewed ale.

She didn't dare to look at Mr. Herbert. Never mind that they had been on first-name basis yesterday. The fair was an incident out of time. Today they would likely be on a formal footing again. Perhaps it was for the best. Why moon over someone who probably wouldn't want you even if he could have you?

By this time Emma was sunk so in her melancholy that not even bracing words from the earl could cheer her.

"Ready, my girl?" he inquired as he paused behind her chair. "You look fine as five pence today."

"Of course, sir. The maid ought to have our things down by now. We will be off in a trice, just you see." She became determinedly cheerful, earning puzzled looks from the young gentlemen and Gussie's worried regard.

They set out for the first of their stops in a gay cavalcade.

It was a golden day in late summer. As the carriages rolled out of Marlborough they could see the White Horse to one side, tidy cottages to the other. Constructed of flint and brick with neatly thatched roofs, they had a warmly welcoming look to them.

Once beyond the town, the gently rolling downs came into view. Further along they saw farmhouses that not only had thatched roofs, but thatched walls, in a few of the farmyards, prosperously echoing the house.

"I'd not like to be crossing here in the winter," the earl mused aloud. "The road is a miry mess. The wind and rain come sweeping across the downs, pelting a man's carriage not to mention his poor beasts, and driving the cold into his bones. Nasty weather here in winter more often than not."

"How nice that we are blessed with good weather, my dear," the countess replied with her imperturbable calm.

"Indeed," the earl answered with a smile.

"How far is it to Avebury?" Emma asked, not wishing to think of the coming winter cold on such a pleasant day. The thought flashed through her mind that it would be just like the previous one—dull and dreary.

"Ben Coachman said it would be six miles, my dear. It won't take us long to get there. What do you intend to do?" The countess looked at Gussie, then Emma with quizzical eyes.

Emma shot a look at Gussie, who had been gazing out of the window at the passing scene. "I should like to see the stones, walk about the area. 'Tis said that the druids once worshiped there. Do you really think that is true?"

"I doubt anyone knows for certain," the countess replied. "Are you feeling quite the thing, Emma? You seem a trifle pale."

"I did not sleep well, likely due to the excitement of actually taking a trip. And such a trip—to go to Bath!"

The countess exchanged a look with her husband, then said in her bland manner, "It is a crying shame that your father keeps you so close to home."

"Indeed, ma'am. My thinking is that he intends to compel me to wed Claude for lack of a suitor. If I meet no other gentleman, there is no competition. What Papa cannot seem to understand is that I will never marry my cousin! I shall remain a spinster instead." Emma faced the countess with a defiant gaze, her chin somewhat raised.

"So you have said time out of mind. But now you have met Mr. Herbert. What a pity he is ineligible."

"And precisely what is wrong with my great-nephew?" the earl demanded to know.

"Money, my dear. The darling boy may be as handsome as can stare, have the nicest of manners, dress in the neatest of taste—Emma's father will not pay the slightest attention to that," she explained. "He wants for property and money."

"Hmpf," the earl retorted. But apparently Lady Stanwell's words had given him food for thought. He remained silent for some minutes while he considered the matter. Whatever conclusion he reached was not shared with the occupants of the carriage, however. He kept his own counsel.

The village of Avebury proved to be naught but a charming handful of houses, a church, and a small inn, plus the manor.

Mr. Herbert joined her in inspecting the area. Avebury Manor could be glimpsed just off the High Street. The tall stones could be viewed from various points on the street as they peered around buildings and trees. Emma guessed there must be around a hundred tall stones standing in the circle, with trees interspersed. She fancied they were around fifteen feet high, some perhaps taller. The circle was girdled by a broad ditch, above which rose a rounded rampart. The road cut through the rampart, neat bridges crossing the ditch.

Gussie and Rawlinson wandered in different directions while the earl and countess, after a brief perusal, remained in the comfort of their traveling carriage. The earl drifted off to sleep while the countess appeared to be deep in thought.

"There seem to be two other smaller circles here," Mr. Herbert said, pointing to double concentric rows of stones. Some stones were upright, some tilted badly, while others had fallen to the ground. They were weathered, but still impressive.

"I am so glad to have seen this. Think of their antiquity. No one knows for sure who created this place or when it was done. Do you suppose it was the druids?" Emma asked.

"I have read it might be even earlier than the druids."

She stared at him, unable to imagine the time before time began. She walked to one of the stones, hesitantly touching the surface that had been somewhat warmed by the sun. "So many years." She smiled at him, shaking her head in bemusement.

"How do you think they managed to bring the stones here, then erect them?" Adam wondered.

"It seems incredible. I imagine it would be difficult to do even today. What a contrast between the grandeur of the stones and the pretty village." She gestured to the nearest cottage.

The sun warmed the earth, a gentle breeze brought the ripe scents of late summer floating on the air. The faint fragrance of small scabious and harebell blooms teased their noses along with the pungency of freshly cut hay in a nearby pasture.

Emma looked up from the stone, its surface worn from centuries of rain and wind, to find Adam Herbert studying her.

"Mr. Herbert, that is, Adam, what think you of all this?"

"I am glad you have not ceased to use my name. As to Avebury circle, I must say it is impressive. I doubt we have anything so splendid near where I live in Kent."

They resumed walking, slowly making their way back along the High Street, totally absorbed in each other, and discussing the possibilities of antiquity.

Emma glanced sideways at him from time to time, wishing he were not so ineligible.

"Do you intend to return to your home in Kent?" she asked.

He sighed. "I should like to find a position as an assistant to a steward or land manager somewhere. I am not sure how to go about it. Perhaps my great-uncle can advise me."

"The earl is a very wise man." They talked a bit more about his future before she continued. "There is no hope of you acquiring property of your own?"

He gave a bark of laughter. "None at all. I suppose I might ask one of my sisters' husbands if they could use an assistant. I hate to do that, though."

"There is such a thing as being too independent, you know."

"You have been listening to Rawlinson. He is all for my petitioning the Marquess of Brentford or Lord Latham for such a post. If worse comes to worse, I may have to do just that."

"But you wish to be independent," she said with a nod.

"You understand?"

"I do. I wish for the same . . . for all the good it does me."

Adam was about to inquire why she wanted independence when Rawlinson called to them.

When Adam and Emma joined the others, they were informed it was but a short distance to Silbury Hill.

"I think it would be great fun to walk over there. You can see it to the south of us for it is immense." Gussie turned to face south, and the others did as well.

"Why do I have the feeling it is further than you suspect?" Emma asked.

"Well . . . In any event, the earl said they would meet

us there. When we are finished investigating that site, we will carry on to Beckhampton Inn," Gussie said with enthusiasm.

Rawlinson gave his boots a dismayed look, then offered his arm to Gussie. "Really, my girl, you are doing me in, you know."

"Poppycock, it will do you good."

They moved off in the vague direction of the enormous earthen mound, gently arguing about the exercise.

Rawlinson paused to speak with the countess at her imperious summons. Gussie held back, looking unsure. There appeared to be a heated discussion before the younger pair took off again.

"I wonder what all that was about?" Emma said slowly.

"We shall find out in due time, I fancy."

Silbury Hill was not all Emma had hoped. For one thing, it was nothing but an enormous hill. It told them nothing. "Not that the Avebury stones gave us that much of a hint as to their beginnings, but this is even more obscure," she said.

"Think of the number of people and the time involved in creating this enormous pile of dirt, my dear," Adam replied.

"I hadn't considered that," Emma admitted. "I wonder what is at the top of the hill."

"Want to find out?" Adam challenged, not for a moment believing she would climb up there.

"I believe I shall." Without a word to anyone, Emma began her ascent to the top of the hill. While it wasn't steep, it was much further than she had thought. She was tiring when she discovered that Adam had joined her. Not about to reveal she was weary, she paused on the faintly level tier mid-way up. "My, you got here quickly." She took a deep breath, then resumed her climb to the top, pushing herself to make it.

"You are the most determined creature," Adam said, just a bit breathless.

They gained the top, a lovely level spot from which one could see for miles, since the day was clear. Below them, the carriages looked like toys. Gussie and Rawlinson stared up, showing no inclination to join them.

"It gives one an eerie feeling of antiquity. All this was done such a long time ago." She pointed to the haphazard circle of stones, then at the other earthworks in the area. "How far up have we climbed, do you think?" Emma asked at last, having had her fill of gazing.

"I should think well over one hundred feet. Now we are here, what do you intend to do?" He was patently amused.

"I shall run to the bottom!" Emma cried, taking one long last look at the surrounding countryside before taking off at a goodly pace. "Catch me if you can!" Her long skirt impeded her run, but still she went at an ever-increasing rate.

"Miss Lawrence, take care!" Adam tore after her, wondering if she was bent on killing herself. First, there had been the incident at the racecourse, and now this. The girl was a menace! He passed her, hoping he could catch her if need be.

He was just in time. At the foot of the hill he reached out his arms, almost going over backwards as she plowed into him. His hands grasped her arms to brace them both.

"Oh!" She leaned against him, scandalously close.

He took note of her charmingly flushed cheeks, the flashing of her deep blue eyes, and the rise and fall of a rather splendid bosom as she sought to regain her breath. Yes, she definitely was a menace.

"You see," she gasped, "I came to no harm."

"You little fool! I think you are determined to do yourself in. It's nothing short of a miracle that you didn't." His expression was grim. "Straighten your pelisse and bonnet, then we can join the Stanwells."

How dare he! Emma simmered with resentment that this man should tell her what she inwardly knew—she had behaved in a hoydenish manner. "It was glorious, almost like flying!" She defied him to deny that it had been a marvelous thing. He said nothing in reply, further provoking her.

Emma adjusted her bonnet, feeling rather foolish now that she had torn down the hill like an utter romp. Perhaps she was more of a madcap than she realized. Or was it her rescuer who brought forth this side of her nature? He didn't have to scold her, though. She glared at him before turning to the others.

Adam escorted her to join Gussie and Rawlinson.

Gussie gave Emma an admonishing look, but merely said, "You will never guess what the countess has planned."

"Tell me," Emma begged, thankful to escape a scolding.

Rawlinson said, "She wants me to invite some friends from Town to the Hall. Perhaps twelve in all."

"Indeed!" Gussie inserted. "Young gentlemen and ladies. They are to remain for at least a week, at the end of which we shall have a ball."

"Oh, my!" Emma cried. "She said something about a ball."

"That means no outrageous doings, my girl," the viscount admonished, the twinkle in his eyes belying any displeasure.

The four young people slowly walked to where the

carriages waited. Nothing more was said about Emma's scandalous dash.

"You are most tolerant of our fancies to wait here while we gawk at the ancient remains," Adam said politely to the earl.

He found himself under his great-uncle's scrutiny as though the earl sought to solve a conundrum of sorts. "We are content to take our ease."

"And nap, as well," the countess added with an amused glance at the earl.

"And Emma, was the climb to the top worth the effort?" the earl asked.

"It was lovely! We could see for miles. You all looked so small." She met Gussie's censorious gaze with a defiant one of her own. "You should have tried it, Gussie."

"Those people were watching a while ago, when you were climbing to the top. They were not kind to you, Emma." Gussie glanced to a group of people nearby.

"Oh, pooh," Emma replied, a bit upset with her dearest friend. Since Rawlinson arrived she had started becoming a pattern-card of propriety. Her old friend was changing before her eyes. She looked at the people, vaguely familiar and seeming very proper.

"Just pray we do not meet them again!" Gussie cautioned.

Emma was about to enter the Stanwell carriage, assisted by Adam. She paused to give Gussie a horrified look. "You do not seriously think we might!"

"I heard them murmur something about Bath. Who knows but what you may see them while there?"

Emma gave Adam a dismayed look, then entered the Stanwell carriage, subsiding in a corner. Gussie followed, while Adam and Rawlinson walked to get into the cabriolet.

Shortly the two carriages left Silbury Hill to return to the main road that ran between Marlborough and Bath by way of Devizes.

Emma wondered if she was totally ruined.

Chapter Nine

The inn at Beckhampton was all they had hoped to find. The countess immediately drew Gussie and Emma along with her, leaving the gentlemen to sample the home-brewed ale available in the private parlor that Rawlinson had bespoke.

"Now, girls," the countess declared once the women were settled in her own little sitting room upstairs. "I had the most splendid notion to have a ball. Rawlinson will invite some of his friends to stay so we can have a proper party. We must have a decent number for it to be a success." She paused, obviously considering the plan. "I believe there are a few young people within a reasonable distance of Stanwell. When we return I shall send off invitations. You may help, Emma. It has been an age since we entertained, but I have not forgotten a thing."

"Ma'am, are you certain you wish to do this?" Emma asked, still somewhat chastened by what had occurred earlier. All the way from Silbury Hill to Beckhampton she had smarted from the set-down Mr. Herbert gave her. It had made the journey most unpleasant for her, short though it was.

"We will stay in Bath long enough for you each to augment your wardrobes. And you both must practice your steps. Do you waltz?" When Gussie shook her head, the countess tsked and said, "Our grandson shall teach you. I truly do not think he will mind in the least. And Emma, you shall practice with our Adam."

The two young women exchanged cautious looks.

"Ma'am," Emma hesitantly said, "I do not think Mr. Herbert is much in charity with me at the moment." It was the most polite way she could point out the difficulty with Lady Stanwell's suggestion. Mr. Herbert appeared to hold Emma in some aversion. He didn't seem like the sort of person to change his mind with any rapidity.

"Pish tosh, he will recover. I do suggest that you attempt to behave yourself, my girl. This hoydenish behavior you have indulged in of late simply will not do." She waggled a finger at Emma, but her smile indicated that she thought the entire matter one that would soon blow over.

Emma could feel the heat rising in her face. The countess was all too correct. While Emma might have done a few silly things in the past, there was something about this very proper gentleman that drove her to daring behavior. She could not seem to help it. Yet, when he scolded her, she felt wretched. Why that might be she didn't know, but it was so. Perhaps it was because he was of a clergyman's family and had thought to enter the ranks of the clergy at one time that she felt compelled to be outrageous. She had wanted to shock him! He must think her a dreadful miss, truly madcap. But she didn't wish him to think ill of her. He was handsome, charming, but alas . . . totally unacceptable.

Gussie reached out to pat Emma on the hand. "I know Emma will be more proper, my lady. She is not given to mad starts as a rule."

Emma squirmed with her annoyance. First Mr. Herbert and now Gussie taking her to task, never mind that

Gussie meant well. Mr. Herbert likely did too. Perhaps she had been allowed free rein too much, as her papa said when he scolded her for some impishness she had done. She did not mean to be outlandish, but there were moments when the lure was irresistible, even if it was not quite the thing to be done. The thought that Mr. Herbert would be scandalized were he to learn of some of her more daring escapades depressed her for at least one minute. Subdued, she turned her thoughts to more agreeable matters.

The countess discussed what sort of clothing ought to be purchased and what other things might be required for the upcoming party. It wasn't long before the girls were caught up in the delight of planning an affair that was bound to be the talk of the area for months to come.

In the comfort of the inn's best private parlor the earl turned to his great-nephew. "Rawlinson tells me that you would like a post as a steward or manager. Is that so?"

Adam admitted that his cousin had spoken the truth. The image of Emma Lawrence danced in his mind a few moments before he dismissed it. It was rather stupid to daydream over the unattainable. A steward, while quite respectable, was not up to courting a lovely lady of obviously superior means.

"There is nothing I would like more than to manage an estate. I find it challenging to experiment with new methods, learn the latest means of improving the soil, better the breeds of animals found on a farm." Adam wondered if the earl thought him slightly foolish to want something so mundane, when the viscount would likely turn his nose up at the same thing. After all, Rawlinson was a prime example of a *ton*-ish gentleman. If anyone could appear to greater advantage, it was beyond Adam to imagine it.

"Hmm," the earl said, studying Adam a bit more before he ventured to reply. "You can apprentice to my man when we return, if that is what you truly wish. Solid future in it. I fancy you have the nous to handle it." The earl rubbed his chin while he considered Adam. "The countess is planning a little party. You and Rawlinson will both contribute your considerable charms to its success."

Adam grinned. "If my cousin will assist my selection, I need to obtain a new waistcoat, perhaps a few neckcloths. He far outshines me, I fear." He gave Rawlinson an admiring glance. "I like his style of dress."

The viscount gave Adam a surprised stare. "Do you, by Jove!"

"Not that I can afford to emulate you to any degree. Your taste might be very fine, but it also takes a bit of blunt," Adam ruefully confessed.

"While you are living with me, I shall undertake to furnish your needs, Adam," the earl declared in his bluff manner. "You can do no better than to seek my grandson's advice. He is always top-of-the-trees in dress as well as breeding."

"Heavens!" Rawlinson cried, raising his tankard of ale as in a toast. "I must return home more often. It is vastly satisfactory to my sometimes wounded spirit."

"And I," the earl added, "intend to buy myself one of those canes with the clouded amber tops. Devilishly fine-looking they are." He also raised his tankard in a toast to the others.

The evening meal was superior, the beds upon which they slept even better than expected. When the group met to break their fast in the morning, all, even Emma, were in the best of moods. Her disgrace of the day before appeared to have been forgotten, or at least set aside.

Emma had donned her straw bonnet with the pretty cluster of cherry ribands on one side. She was pulling on her York tan gloves before leaving the inn when she encountered the people she had spotted the day before just after she had made her scandalous dash down Silbury Hill. They looked straight through her. She hadn't expected to be greeted with friendliness, but she had met them at one time in the past. They should know who she was. They could have been civil. It rather crushed her to be so treated, especially in front of the countess.

The countess was right behind her. When she glanced at the strangers, it turned out they knew who she was.

"Lady Stanwell! How lovely to see you again. It has been an age, has it not?" the older lady gushed.

Her ladyship studied the foursome. She nodded with civility. "We are on our way to Bath. I intend to oversee the shopping for my dear young neighbors. When we hold our ball, I want them both to be in first looks."

The four looked uncomfortable. The older woman, who reminded the countess that she was Lady Tate, managed a smile for Gussie. The others hurried off.

"I wonder how they feel now?" the countess murmured, as she left the inn with Emma and Gussie at her side. "They have given Emma the cut direct, then learned you are a part of my group, under my protection. I am of a mind to send them an invitation just to make them squirm!"

"I know them slightly. I expect I have given them a disgust of me. It is a price I do not mind in the least—they are toad-eaters of the first degree." Emma attempted a smile, but suspected it was more of a grimace.

Mr. Herbert and the viscount led the way south into the market town of Devizes with the cabriolet, while the earl's traveling carriage followed at a sedate pace.

Emma looked out of the window to the east of the road where the mysterious Silbury Hill loomed in the distance. The site of her disgrace did not bring happy memories. She pushed the recollection of the feel of Mr. Herbert's muscular body out of her mind. A young lady wasn't supposed to dwell on anything so improper. No matter—it lingered anyway, along with a number of others, like his slow smile, those beautiful gray eyes, and the richness of his auburn hair.

Lord and Lady Stanwell kept up a quiet commentary on the countryside, supposedly for the edification of the girls, neither of whom paid a great deal of attention.

"Bishops Canning is off to our left along here," the earl advised. "We will change horses in Devizes, then be off."

"To Bath," Emma concluded respectfully.

"To Bath," repeated Gussie, with her delight evident in her voice. "What sort of gown will you order, Emma? For the ball, that is?"

"I think she would look well in an oyster-white satin," the countess said in a sleepy voice. "And she needs a rose-sprigged muslin, perhaps a French cambric in blue. Maybe a gown of India mull as well. I believe lavender would be nice."

"I have never had so many new gowns at one time in my life," Emma said, taking a deep breath at the very thought of new dresses. Not only dresses, but parasols, reticules, pretty leather slippers, and a new pair of half-boots. Bonnets, of course, were a necessity. "I trust there are any number of fine millinery shops in Bath?" She eyed the countess with hope.

"There are millinery shops, seamstresses, and other shops such as I doubt you have ever seen, my girl. You may obtain a variety of slippers just your size and bespoke half-boots to be ready in days," the countess replied as the carriage rolled into the Devizes coaching inn where a change of horses was accomplished in minutes. From there on it seemed as though the miles dragged past them, yet Emma knew full well that it was because she was impatient to see Bath again. Not that she remembered one bit of it, since she had been all of four years old the last time. Still, she recalled the event with the happiness of a child who had been indulged with a gaily painted rocking horse. It was one of the last things her Mama had bought her.

When at last they rolled over the remaining hill and down into the lushly green valley where the charming city of Bath gleamed in the late summer sun, Emma and Gussie sighed with relief and something akin to pure joy.

Emma was certain that she couldn't possibly get into any trouble in such a lovely city. What could likely happen?

The proprietor of the White Hart Inn bowed reverently to the Earl and Countess of Stanwell, Viscount Rawlinson, the two appealing young women, and the earl's handsome great-nephew, Mr. Herbert, sending each party to their assigned rooms with a suitably impressed footman.

Late July was about the end of the summer season, yet far removed from the winter season in Bath. The town was thin of exalted company, but then, the peerage didn't come to Bath in the numbers they once had. The proprietor rubbed his hands, only too delighted to pass along the identity of his new guests to anyone who might happen to inquire.

The countess paused before the door that led to the room to be shared by Emma and Gussie. "We have a private parlor adjacent to our room. Join us once you are settled, and we shall enjoy a fine dinner that Rawlinson has ordered for our delectation." She gave Emma a searching look quite as though she was about to caution her against any foolishness. Nothing was said, however, to Emma's relief. The countess and earl went on to their rooms while the two girls whisked around the door into the privacy allotted them.

Once in their room, Emma clasped Gussie's hands to dance about the room. "We are here! Oh, Gussie, we are actually in Bath! I vow I do not know what to look for first, but oh, to go to the shops first thing in the morning—dresses, bonnets, slippers, reticules—all out there just waiting for us!"

Gussie dropped hands to walk over to the window that looked out on the quiet street below. Mellow light cast shadows across the street from the many lanterns on the front of the elegant inn. "The Abbey is straight through from here, and the Pump Room is closer to Stall Street—on the right side of the Abbey Churchyard," Gussie said. "Shall we be obliged to sample the water, do you suppose?" She made a face at the thought.

"I think not. You made good use of your time in the carriage with a *Guide to Bath* in your hands. Only tell me where the shopping is the best, and we can repair to that street come morning."

"Oh, Milsom Street, my dear," Gussie replied with a laugh. "And what sort of millinery do you wish, miss?" she continued, imitating the sort of voice one would hear in the better shops.

"A dashing bonnet of . . . oh, what is best, Gussie?"

Emma wished she had paid more attention to the copies of *La Belle Assembleé* the countess possessed. The illustrations were helpful, but what she needed were the latest details of fashion.

"Leghorn, I imagine. I cannot begin to tell you what we will find." She continued to stare at the view, her thoughts private, until she gave herself a shake, turning aside.

Emma spun around from their window, allowing the draperies to fall and thus obscure them from prying eyes. "I wonder what Mr. Herbert and the viscount will do? I fancy Mr. Herbert is anxious to obtain a waistcoat with the viscount's advice, and did he not also mention neckcloths?"

"Men," Gussie said with a laugh and a nod as one who had several brothers. "You may rest assured that Mr. Herbert will be decked out in the finest Bath has to offer. As will we, dear Emma. Never forget the ball the countess has promised us."

"And we are to practice the waltz!"

Dinner found the two young ladies full of suppressed excitement. The countess languidly composed lists that both of the girls thought excessive, if vastly delightful.

The earl and the two younger men discussed where one might obtain an acceptable waistcoat.

"Mind you," the viscount mused, "you would do far better in London. I fear the tailoring here might be a trifle provincial."

"I think you are too nice in your tastes, Rawlinson," the earl replied. "There is nothing wrong with a respectable tailor here in Bath. Prices are bound to be lower, too."

The countess glanced at him, then back to the young

ladies. "That applies to us as well. You shall be pleased with the cost of a gown here compared to Town."

"And what do you intend to purchase?" Mr. Herbert inquired.

"Everything possible," Emma replied simply. "I need so much. The dressmaker in the village tries her best, but her best leaves something to be desired, sir." She thought she caught a glimpse of admiration in his eyes, but the soft light afforded by the candles made it impossible to know for certain.

"I imagine that Lady Tate and her party will go into a rented establishment. He might be no more than a baronet, but he seems to have money, and I suppose they intend to remain for a time. Lord Tate does not look at all well. Gout, I should suspect. I fancy he will take the waters." Lady Stanwell turned to Emma, "And where did you meet her, my dear?"

"There was an assembly in Pewsey that she chanced to attend when I was also there. Remember, Gussie? Your mother took us."

"Indeed, I do. How could I forget? That was the time you consumed three glasses of punch that had been tampered with by some young bucks." Gussie fixed her gaze on the countess. "It did not sit well with Emma, I fear."

Emma was not about to dwell on a humiliation of the past. "Where shall we go first come morning?"

"A dressmaker, I believe. I know of one who does very well and has an adequate staff so your gowns can be made up quickly. Since it is late summer, her patronage will be down. No doubt she will be pleased to get a few orders."

Visions of oyster-white satin trimmed with fringe and other confections of fashion danced in Emma's head.

The earl suggested an early night. Seeing that the man who must be rising seventy would be tired after a day of traveling, no matter how leisurely they went, Emma and Gussie immediately proposed they retire.

Once the earl and countess had gone to their room, Emma and Gussie rose to leave as well.

"I do not see why we couldn't play cards. Your maid can remain with us," the viscount pointed out. He promptly sent for the maid while Mr. Herbert found a deck of cards.

"I must say I was not ready to go to my rest," Gussie said, her high spirits evident in the sparkle in her eyes.

When the maid had taken a seat on the far side of the room, the viscount dealt out the cards and they began a game of whist.

Later Mr. Herbert declared, "It is a good thing we played for penny points. I'd not have a shilling to my name. I had no notion you were so expert at cards, Miss Lawrence. You trounced us!" His smile took away any sting his words might have held.

"I believe that since we are part of a family group we could overlook the formalities. Emma and Gussie, do you have any objections?" The viscount looked from one to the other.

Emma took note of Gussie's shy grin and the twinkle in Mr. Herbert's fine gray eyes and nodded her agreement. While she and Mr. Herbert had once agreed to be informal, after her scandalous dash down the hill he had returned to a more proper mode of address. She wondered if this meant she was forgiven. She hoped so, for it was vastly uncomfortable to be on tenterhooks all the time, wanting to call him Adam but hesitant to seem forward.

"It is settled." He scooped up the cards to stow them away. "Where do we go first in the morning, then?"

"We are to the dressmaker," Emma reminded. "And I fancy you will look for the best tailor Bath has to offer."

"And may we cross paths at some point. It would not do for you to be here and miss a confectionery shop. And I intend to obtain tickets to the theater for us all. While the theater will close in August, there are still enough visitors in Bath to encourage the production of plays."

"Famous!" Emma cried softly so as not to disturb the earl and countess. She rose from where she had been seated. "I think we had best get some sleep. Morning has much to offer."

They quietly left the neat sitting room, their Nancy following the young ladies to their room down the hall. The countess had arranged for her to sleep on a truckle bed, so as to be nearby if needed. Emma examined the lock on her door and wondered if the maid was more for protection.

Nancy assisted them with their clothes. Once in bed, Gussie looked over to where Emma was propped against her pillows. "We are really here."

Emma raised her brows. "Indeed. Oh, Gussie, what an adventure!"

"Emma," Gussie said, with a doubtful look, "I could swear I saw Claude today."

"I thought I saw him in Marlborough. Haven't seen him since, though. I cannot think why he would tag after us."

"Perhaps he is interested in keeping an eye on you? After all, he has a vested interest in seeing that you remain single. He depends on your father to unite you with him in matrimony to keep him from *point non plus.*"

Emma grimaced. "What could he do? It is hardly

likely that I could marry anyone while on a trip to Bath."

"You might become engaged."

"To whom? Rawlinson and I do not suit. Mr. Herbert, Adam, that is, thinks I am a heedless ninny. Am I supposed to draw a betrothal from out of nowhere? What a fool Claude is."

Gussie drew her feet up, leaning her chin against her well-covered knees. "We had best be on our guard."

"Rubbish! He wouldn't dare try anything in Bath."

"All the same, take care."

Emma didn't reply, just blew out the candle to leave the room in the dim light offered by the lanterns outside the inn.

She remained awake for a time, however.

She had tucked the small gun her father had given her last year into her valise, thinking it might be useful. One never knew what might happen when traveling. From now on, she would tuck it into her leather reticule. It was a pity the weather was so mild. It would have been so simple to conceal it in a muff.

Her dreams were haunted by shadowy, muffled figures, dark carriages that went all too fast, screams in the night. It was little wonder that when she woke she felt out of sorts. That lasted until she remembered where she was and why.

"Gussie, wake up. Today we are to go shopping!"

Chapter Ten

Over a dainty bit of sustenance, Lady Stanwell outlined her plans for the day. To her awed audience of two young ladies, she said that the dressmaker had been sent a message to be ready for them, prepared for a substantial order. Then they were to proceed to the premier shoe- and boot-maker of Bath, where they would purchase the neat flat-heeled shoes both desired, at least half a dozen pair each, and order several pairs of half-boots.

"I am reliably informed there are some charming gauzes to be found in a shop on Bath Street, where we may also find the most perfect lace for only twenty shillings an ell." Lady Stanwell again checked her list.

Emma exchanged a guarded look with Gussie. Of a sudden she realized that her precious quarterly allowance plus what she had not spent from the previous quarter wouldn't go as far as she hoped.

"I hope neither of you has any silly ideas about stinting on your shopping. Both of you need so many things. The earl will pay for all, and you can settle with him later. You, dear Emma, are woefully lacking in fashionable garments."

Visibly relieved, Emma said all would be as her ladyship desired. Her father would pay the bills, gladly or not, for he would never want to be beholden to the earl.

Gussie's father had previously made arrangements with the earl.

Rawlinson and Mr. Herbert joined them, with the earl setting aside his copy of the most recent issue of the *Bath Herald*. The three men settled comfortably into the vacant chairs by the table. The viscount apologized for their tardy arrival, explaining that his valet had been teaching Herbert a new manner of arranging his neckcloth.

Mr. Herbert looked a trifle embarrassed at this attention to his attire, but Emma noted he appeared most handsome this morning. The cravat was a great success from what she could tell—restrained yet refined. She was aware that the different styles had been given names—like the mathematical, *Trone d'Amour*, and the oriental. She had to confess she didn't know one from another. To her, a neckcloth was merely a strip of linen that swathed the neck. She knew most gentlemen gave a lot of attention to the style of their cravat, and from what she had seen, some were utterly ridiculous.

"I am greatly in debt to Rawlinson and Hilton for their attempts to create me a fashionable gentleman." He spoke with gentle irony in his voice, which Emma could not help but admire. He was not a man given to pretensions.

"You look very dashing," the countess pronounced after a quick perusal of her great-nephew.

There was a comfortable aroma of coffee and warm rolls, bacon, and other breakfast favorites lingering in the room. It was apparent that the men had not been the least impressed by their journey into the elegant town of Bath. Their genial talk was of tailors and waistcoat styles, colors and fabrics, not terribly unlike the women in their quest for fashions. Only they spoke of stripes versus patterns, a good white Marcella as opposed to fine kerseymere or tasteful cashmere.

"For evening black or white is preferred," instructed the viscount. "For day you might select a rich green or buff with blue stripes—which I rather favor if the stripes are neat and narrow. A dark blue or bronze would go well with your hair."

Emma took surreptitious peeks at Mr. Herbert. Why was she so affected by the mere sight of him when he appeared to have not the slightest reaction to her? She would take care not to let him know how she reacted to the mere sight of him!

She set about pouring tea or coffee while Gussie passed toast, jam, and anything else wanted. The servants had been dismissed, the group preferring to serve themselves.

Emma decided it best not to look at Mr. Herbert, fearful that she might reveal too much. Her father would never permit an alliance with him, no matter he was the earl's great-nephew.

"I doubt we shall see you men until late in the afternoon," the countess said. "I will need to put my feet up after a round of shopping. I fancy the girls can be trusted to wander through the bookseller's on Milsom Street. It is No. 43, I believe." She glanced at her notes, then nodded her prettily capped head. "Indeed. I should like a nice novel by that lady who wrote *Sense and Sensibility* if you can find such a one. Today or tomorrow—we shall see how our time goes."

"We would be most happy to hunt it out for you," Emma offered, thinking that it was the very least she might do for her patroness.

"I intend to look in at the Pump Room and sign the subscription book," the earl said. "Will you stop in there as well, Sophia?"

"Naturally. There might be someone we know in town. I will look over the list of newcomers." She smiled fondly at her husband before rising from the table. "Come, girls. We have much to do."

The trio collected their bonnets, reticules, and, in particular, parasols, as one never knew when it might come on to rain in Bath. As they left the inn bound for Milsom Street, Emma took note of the fashionable people around. While Bath was not the metropolis that London was, it was a sizable city, still drawing the stylish as well as the infirm who sought the hot baths and the water to cure their ills. Most of the people were older, though. The young ladies glanced curiously at the Pump Room as they passed. Once on Milsom Street, they passed bow-fronted shops full of enticing goods. Bonnets beckoned, shawls cast lures, and one shop in particular with cleverly designed reticules and gloves promised to fulfill all their desires, not to mention needs.

At the dressmaker's establishment it didn't take long for the girls to realize that this was not to be a simple business. The styles had to be selected, then a fabric of suitable weight, color, and weave chosen. The countess might be past sixty, but she was knowledgeable to a fine degree and had as much energy as did the girls. Emma guessed that if the countess were selecting gowns for herself, she would have summoned the dressmaker to her rooms at the White Hart. The shop offered a far greater choice of fabrics for them.

When they entered the shop, Gussie had glanced about the interior with its little gilt chairs and soft gray carpeting with an awed mien. This was far from the village seamstress!

Emma gave her a warning shake of her head. With the countess directing their shopping expedition, there was no point in taking anything amiss. The stack of pattern cards brought for their inspection brought a sparkle of anticipation to the eyes of both girls.

"Emma first, then you, dear Gussie." The countess turned to the owner of the select establishment with an inquiry about the quality of the mull. Rolls of various mulls were fetched for selection, and the countess chose with unerring taste.

Lady Stanwell desired to have the lilac India mull made up first, then a stylish design in French cambric. "Blue, I believe, as your eyes are blue and the color goes so well with your skin," she said to Emma after casting a look at her.

The lilac India mull was to be a round dress and have four narrow flounces edged with blond lace on the skirt and elegant full sleeves with lace trimming in a clever design. Several rows of tucks added to the charm of the blue cambric dress. Over the simple dress would be worn a tasteful spencer of white satin with blue puffs on the top of the sleeves and blue ribands across the bosom. The spencer's design allowed a pretty lace ruff to fall over it around the neck.

"Make notes, dear girl," the countess urged. "Blue half-boots with this dress and shoes of pale lilac kid for the mull."

Emma scribbled hastily, adding her own ideas for bonnets and gloves, not to forget parasols and shawls.

When Lady Stanwell pointed to the illustration of her special gown for the ball, Emma swallowed with care. She had never in her life worn anything so utterly beautiful. The oyster satin chosen was to hang in a simple straight line to the floor, and the brief tucked bodice and short full sleeves were to be ornamented with point lace. It was utterly breathtaking.

"A cashmere shawl with this, my dear. The weather

has been so tiresome this summer. I declare I never did put away my warmer pelisse."

The countess spotted the drawing of a perfectly charming white muslin that was far from being insipid. She added that to the growing list.

When it became Gussie's turn, the colors were rich peach, pale jonquil, and a delicate sea-green. The colors and fabrics brought out hitherto unsuspected lights in Gussie's hair. The countess dismissed the notion that Gussie ought to wear the white favored by the young girls making their bows to society. "Nonsense," she declared. "White would be a disaster with that hair. We shall keep the designs proper, but color you must have. You might look well in that almond sarcenet."

An hour and a half later, feeling as though she had been swept up by a strong wind, Emma thought longingly of a nice cup of tea, with perhaps some ginger biscuits.

The young ladies left the shop in a semidaze. Compared to selecting gowns, choosing boots and slippers would be a snap. Softest kid shoes in various shades, simple white and blue satin dancing slippers, and sturdy jean half-boots in deep blue and warm brown were swiftly selected.

"I had no idea we might find shoes and boots to fit," Emma murmured to Gussie, who was trying on a pair of peach kid Roman sandals.

Gussie merely bestowed a bemused smile on her friend and went on picking out her shoes and boots. Both girls were glad to sit down for a bit. It was surprising how tiring shopping could be—even when it was for something desired.

The countess sat with a cup of tea offered by the proprietor for his august patron. She said little, but kept a sharp eye on everything selected.

The shop owner assured them that all the items would be delivered to the White Hart with dispatch. That the earl would settle the bill was not said but definitely understood.

"Let us take a moment for a cup of tea and perhaps some scones at Mollands. They have excellent scones," the countess said. The sun warmed the late morning air. Various shop owners had placed outside their shops urns with flowers blooming in them. It produced a colorful and most delightful aspect.

"Look, ma'am." Gussie urged. "The earl, Mr. Herbert, and Rawlinson are coming our way."

Emma paused while admiring a bonnet to survey the approaching gentlemen. They looked well satisfied with their day to this point.

"Lady Stanwell, Miss Lawrence, and Miss Dunlop, how do you fare?" Mr. Herbert asked with a gentlemanly bow, precisely correct.

"The girls will perish if we do not have a cup of tea. Come, join us at Mollands. I expect the girls will enjoy a taste of something sweet with their tea." The countess waved them all forward. The two young men promptly joined Gussie and Emma, while the earl escorted his wife.

Emma flashed a look at Mr. Herbert, now at her side. She would bet that waistcoat was surely one she hadn't seen yet. It would never do to ask, but she did admire his taste.

She clung to her parasol as the distant rumble of thunder rolled through the valley, hoping that the rain would hold off until they had completed the shopping for this day. The countess had indicated that they would be shopping for several days, and rain would possibly curtail activities.

They chatted with an amiability that drew smiles from the others in the little shop.

Mr. Herbert managed to slip close to Emma, something that sent her pulse racing much faster than warranted by a mere scone and a cup of tea.

"Both Rawlinson and I swear we saw your cousin this morning," he confided. "He was sauntering along the upper end of Milsom Street. I have no idea where he was headed, nor can I imagine where he is staying—unless he is putting up at one of the lodging houses in Bath. We checked York House and he is not registered there."

Emma's heart sank. Mr. Herbert didn't seek her company, he merely wished to pass along some information. "That was most kind of you. He is certainly persistent in his pursuit, is he not?" Emma tried to smile and suspected it appeared a trifle forced. "Unless, like us, he has merely come to do a bit of shopping."

"Possibly. His clothes indicate that he does not patronize a London tailor." His voice was dry, although he gave no sign of being contemptuous.

"He ever appears the town beau, however," Emma said thoughtfully, wondering who paid his bills, since he certainly was always pockets-to-let as far as she knew. She suspected her father did the pretty as far as Claude was concerned. While Papa could easily stand buff for his bills, it irked her that her cousin couldn't manage his income better. He was far from being a pauper! She thought his father was reasonably plump in the pocket, although Papa had muttered something about his gambling.

She set aside thoughts of her cousin for discussion on the day's work. "You had success?"

Mr. Herbert nodded politely. "I find creating a polished look more dear than I expected. Rawlinson insists

I must hold up the family name. It would appear the Herbert family is well known in these parts. He said it would pain him beyond belief were I to disgrace the name with an inferior waistcoat."

"Pity Claude's family doesn't feel the same way," Emma replied. "Think how he might be improved!"

Adam choked on a bite of scone. He felt sorry for the young Miss Lawrence. That she should be saddled with a cousin the likes of Claude Polkinghorne was the outside of enough.

He listened to the banter among those at the table. Rawlinson seemed to be more and more attracted to Miss Dunlop. Since she came from a respectable family well known to the earl, moreover blessed with an adequate dowry, Adam supposed it would not be opposed. She would know everyone in the area and be familiar with the customs. Since Rawlinson had spent much of his time in London, it would be helpful to him if his wife was a local woman likely to be accepted by all.

"By the way," the viscount said in a manner that garnered attention at the little table, "I have tickets for a play tomorrow night for us all."

Adam smiled at the look of delight on Emma's face. It was as though someone had handed her a gift. "You are pleased?"

"I have pulled caps with him in the past. I won't anymore. It was most thoughtful of him. Is it not amazing how boys can become considerate gentlemen when grown?" She peered at the viscount with a tolerant gaze.

"Perhaps it would make him a more acceptable spouse?" Adam daringly inquired.

She shook her head, offering Adam a grimace. "No, we would be at odds in no time at all. If I must wed, I should like to have a marriage like that of the earl and his countess. They are fond of each other even after all this time." She cast a warm glance at the countess who was quizzing her grandson about the play they were to see.

"Yes, my parents have such a marriage as well. From what I have seen, my sisters—save for Claudia—married for affection."

"And Claudia?"

The question was polite, so he knew if he chose not to answer, she would not be offended. Still, he hedged.

"If you would rather not reply, I will understand. I am inclined to be curious." She spoke softly, with sensitivity.

"It's not a deep secret. In fact, I would wager that it is all too common. She made what is called an advantageous marriage. Her portion was small, so she had little hope of a grand alliance. The baronet was wealthy and desired a mother for his small son. I feel certain she's been a good mother to him."

"But it has been less than blissful?"

"So I understand," Adam said with a nod. "Unfortunately Lord Fairfax was killed. They had no children together."

"What a pity. Still, she will give his son the best of care, I feel sure." She placed her hand close to his, quite as though she would console him if possible.

Adam cocked a brow in question at this broad statement.

"If she is anything like you, she must be very kind."

He felt an astonishing sensation of pleasure. The encomium of such a nature from Emma was more than he hoped to know.

The rain that had been foreshadowed by the thunder began to pour down with the suddenness that often comes with a late summer rain, bringing exclamations of dismay from all.

"Well, we cannot remain here much longer. See if you can summon several chairs for us, Rawlinson," the countess demanded in her pretty manner. "We shall go to the Pump Room. Perhaps we shall find a few friends and we may visit."

So the group dispersed. The ladies and the earl all went to the Pump Room. Once there, the earl and countess spotted a number of acquaintances.

"Rainy out, what?" he said to his dear wife as they shook their out clothes once inside. "Successful day, I'll be bound."

"Yes, indeed. We shall be inundated with parcels of all sorts."

Emma and Gussie declined a sample of the famous Bath spring water, deciding they would stroll about the room while the older people visited.

"Tomorrow we will have the pleasure of shopping for bonnets and shawls," Gussie said, quietly, lest her enthusiasm be deemed unladylike.

"And reticules as well. Oh, this is pure, pure joy," Emma added, but thinking of the quiet conversation that she had held with Adam Herbert. They managed to get along once in a while. What a pity Claude couldn't be like Mr. Herbert. Were that the case, she would marry Claude at once.

"You look downcast," Gussie said thoughtfully. "What is troubling you—if anything can when we are in Bath and shopping to our heart's content?"

"I have been made more aware of my future. Somehow marriage to Claude is more repugnant than ever."

"Can't you stand firm? Surely your father will not compel you to marry your cousin!" Gussie showed all the sympathy one could wish, giving Emma a concerned look.

"Mr. Herbert said he is certain they spotted Claude at the upper end of Milsom Street this morning. He is such a sneaky creature. What can he be plotting?"

"Rubbish!" Gussie said a trifle loudly. At the dismayed look from an elderly matron, she blushed. "You are under the protection of Lord and Lady Stanwell."

"You are right, of course," Emma said to reassure herself as well as Gussie.

The rain had lessened to a mere mist when Adam Herbert and Rawlinson bustled into the Pump Room, three other young men with them. They came directly to where a very curious Gussie and Emma stood close to the Stanwells.

"I would have you meet three fine fellows, particular friends of mine from Oxford." Rawlinson turned to the three gentlemen. "This is Mr. Algernon Jameson, Sir George Egerton, and Mr. Vincent Ives. Algie lives close to Bath. The others were visiting. Decided to come to Bath for the day." He turned to his grandmother, adding, "I've invited them to visit, ma'am. Knew you would be pleased. I believe you know their parents."

The countess graciously smiled, offering her hand to each in turn. "Algernon's grandmother and I came out together. And everyone of note knows the Egerton and Ives families."

Emma vowed to learn about them all later on. Mr. Jameson had the same color hair as Gussie, and blushed just as easily. Sir George Egerton was a polished gentleman with fine blond hair and blue eyes, with only a hint of the town beau about him, whereas Vincent Ives, his dark hair neatly brushed and gray eyes casting a warm smile her way, was a top-of-the-trees dandy, but seemed nice for all that.

"I mentioned that you intend to have a ball, and they were all for that." Rawlinson grinned at his grandmother.

"My sister Amelia is in Bath to shop. I daresay she would enjoy meeting Miss Lawrence and Miss Dunlop," Mr. Jameson said, with only a faint reddening of his cheeks.

"Excellent. If she knows of two other young ladies who might like to join our little party, do let me know," the countess said with the imperturbability for which she was known.

This was quickly solved when a pretty young lady with dark russet hair and Mr. Jameson's green eyes stepped into the Pump Room with a woman shadowing her, obviously her maid. She made directly for her brother, her face revealing her curiosity.

"Amelia, come meet these friends."

She was a prettily behaved young lady, delighted to meet new people and agog at the idea of being invited to a party at Stanwell Hall. "I am delighted, Lady Stanwell. I do so love a party. Life can be sadly flat when in the country."

"If you have two friends you can recommend for our little party, please let me know. We shall most likely be here for two weeks. It takes time to have gowns made up and all the details attended. Which reminds me, I must go to the shop where I always buy my tea. I promised Gussie's mother to obtain a pound of her favorite Hyson for her. I shall want to inspect what is available as well. Quality tea is most important."

Emma allowed this absentminded reminder to sail past her head. Rather, she went forward to chat with Miss Jameson, finding her charming and unassuming. She also noted that the pretty Miss Jameson cast admiring eyes on none other than Mr. Herbert! Emma might not be able to engage the gentleman, but perverse as women are wont to be, she did not take kindly to having him attached to the pretty and obviously well-to-do Miss Jameson.

"The countess asked if you could think of two young women who might join us," Emma said, with a question in her voice. "I think it will be a fine party, more so with you and your brother, the others as well."

"Louisa Fancourt and Jane Mytton are my dearest friends and live just east of Bath. I know they would adore coming. They both know Sir George and Mr. Ives, and I believe they met the viscount once as well." She paused, casting her gaze to one gentleman in particular. "Mr. Herbert is a stranger, but he seems most admirable," she added shyly.

For some odd reason Emma had all she could do not to snap at the pretty Miss Jameson. "How fortunate we came to Bath to shop. This promises to be a splendid party."

Sir George and Mr. Ives wandered over to engage the three young ladies in conversation. Gussie sparkled at the attention from Mr. Jameson, and Emma admitted an inner delight at the attentiveness showered on her by Sir George.

Adam Herbert joined them, chatting away with Miss Jameson with an ease that annoyed Emma far too much. She couldn't have him, so why did it annoy her so to see him smiling and talking with another young lady?

The party and ball she had looked forward to of a sudden assumed an altogether different character. Perhaps she had some growing up to do, as Gussie's mother had implied from time to time, particularly after the episode with the tampered punch. Although *that* was hardly her fault. It seemed as though trouble seemed to dog her steps far too often.

Emma wished she had her harp to play. She often turned to it when problems beset her. Another glance at Miss Jameson and Adam Herbert revealed that difficulties were ahead.

Outside the thunder rumbled again, fading some as the little storm passed away. Emma wished her troubles would fade away as easily.

Chapter Eleven

The evening passed much the same as the previous one. The earl and countess retired early, and the four younger members of the party played whist for penny points. This time, Adam Herbert did smashingly well.

"I see you profit by previous errors," Rawlinson drawled, while putting a few coins before his cousin.

Gussie chuckled while placing her coins beside the viscount's. Emma added her mite to the little pile before Adam. The modest pile of pence brought obvious gratification to the gentleman in question.

"I doubt it will purchase me a thing, but it is a satisfaction to beat such knowing ones," Adam retorted, grinning at the others. He scooped up his winnings with obvious delight. He gave Emma a sly smile before pushing his chair away from the table. "Perhaps I should become a cardsharp? I could win enough to buy myself an estate."

Emma replied with composure, "Pity we didn't play for pound points, Adam would have had enough for a new coat." As soon as the words were out of her mouth she wished them unsaid. How could she be so cruel as to comment on his garb! What was it about this man that turned her into an unthinking idiot? While his coats were not of the highest style, they were neatly tailored and fit him well. He chose sensible colors, like hunter green and dark gray, that stood well the rigors of traveling without a valet. She felt an utter fool.

Adam glanced at the girl beside him, wondering if she hinted that he needed a new coat. Then he thought again. He doubted if she would be so unfeeling. Still, he couldn't deny a new coat would be most welcome. Yet the blush that now stained her cheeks indicated she felt embarrassment at her words.

"I believe the earl said something about wanting a new coat for you," Rawlinson said quietly. "He is quite proud of you, you know. I believe he wants to show you off. While he is rather gruff at times, I have found in him a pleasing affection. Do not deny him the pleasure of giving you a new coat if he so wishes."

Adam compressed his mouth, wanting to say he would not accept charity, yet the thought of offending his great-uncle held him back. And, he had to confess that it would be agreeable to parade around in a decent coat of Bath cloth—perhaps dark blue, which seemed to be a favored color. So he gave Rawlinson a rueful smile and nodded. "If that is his wish, I will not reject the offer."

The young gentlemen watched Emma and Gussie hurry to their room, then went to explore the city, which Rawlinson assured Adam had not much to offer at night.

"Nothing like London," he declared as they slipped down the stairs and walked off to investigate late-night Bath.

The following day was exceedingly satisfying to Gussie and Emma as far as shopping was concerned. Reticules and parasols, bonnets and shawls all found ready purchasers when the party from Peetbridge strolled along Milsom and Bond streets, admiring the goods in the various bowfronted shop windows.

Lady Stanwell spotted the perfect shawl to drape over the oyster-white ball gown for Emma. And Gussie reveled in a peach-bloom cashmere shawl for her gown.

Emma gratified her newly developed sense of style with a reticule of tucked rose satin for evening and a neat blue plush for day. Gussie was equally lucky to find just what pleased.

At the bookshop they found copies of *Emma* and *Pride and Prejudice* to satisfy Lady Stanwell. The bookseller explained they were out of *Mansfield Park*, but should be receiving more copies shortly. The lady writer was identified as a Miss Austen. "It is to be hoped she will write more novels of such common sense," the clerk said with a thoughtful nod. "It is said she has lived here in Bath, although I cannot say I ever took note of her." Thus he dismissed the author of the entertaining novels the girls looked forward to reading.

They were just about to leave the congenial environs of the bookshop when who entered but their new acquaintance and two young women.

"Miss Jameson! What a nice surprise!" Emma extended her hand in greeting, with Gussie beaming her cheerful smile on all.

Amelia Jameson spoke first. "Permit me to introduce Miss Louisa Fancourt and Miss Jane Mytton. They looked forward to meeting you both. Ah, you have bought three of my favorite books. You will like them prodigiously well. I have come to obtain a copy of *Children of the Abbey*. Louisa says it is too, too chilling!"

Emma explained that Lady Stanwell wished to add the Austen books to her library and made no comments on chilling tales. She enjoyed a good story, but wondered at the title.

"Have you been shopping?" Louisa Fancourt asked. "I vow I adore shopping, especially in Bath. You can find anything here, and less expensive than in London, or so Mama says."

Jane Mytton nodded. "Do you attend the theater this evening? I believe we are to go. Mrs. Jameson said as much."

"Does Mr. Herbert attend as well? And the viscount?" Amelia wondered with a shy smile.

"Rawlinson arranged for our box, so I fancy they will be there with us," Emma replied with as much composure as she could summon. It was plain to her that Amelia had her eyes on Mr. Herbert. Emma wondered if she ought to tell Amelia that the man she admired had little future other than as a steward or agent for some large landowner. Then she decided it would be presumptuous of her to do such a thing. Merely because Amelia admired him did not mean she wished marriage!

The five young women promised to try to see one another if at all possible that evening. Not at all acquainted with the theater, Emma thought it unlikely.

They bid their new friends farewell for the nonce and returned to the White Hart. Here they settled down in the pleasant sitting room. They had exhausted the shops and likely Lady Stanwell as well. Tea and biscuits were brought up to fortify them until dinner might be served.

"I vow, I would not believe peach bloom to be your color, Gussie, but that shawl is amazingly wonderful on you." Emma held up the ravishing length of cashmere for admiration.

Gussie blushed and remarked on Emma's purchases, then she helped serve the tea. The countess put up her feet on a neat little footstool and relaxed against the wing chair.

"Is it not amazing how a cup of tea can restore one, no matter how fatigued?" the countess said after a satisfying sip. "Tomorrow evening we will attend the assembly. There is some sort of entertainment here nearly every night. We have the theater to enjoy this evening. And even if your new dresses are not ready, you will have a fine reticule and shawl as well as new slippers to wear."

Gussie and Emma nodded in happy agreement.

"We shall see our new friends this evening," Gussie said. "Amelia Jameson introduced us to Louisa Fancourt and Jane Mytton at the bookstore. They seem like rather nice young women and . . ." She ceased speaking at the sound of footsteps in the hall outside the room.

The door opened to admit Adam Herbert and Rawlinson, with the earl close behind them. The countess ordered more tea and biscuits as well. The earl chose a glass of sherry.

It was at once obvious that Adam was the recipient of a fine new coat of blue Bath cloth. It seemed that a gentleman had been compelled to depart Bath without it. Only a bit of alteration was required to make it a good fit for Adam. The slight changes had been done so he could have it for the evening ahead. The men had completed their shopping, returning to the tailor shop to find the coat ready for Adam to wear.

They compared notes on their purchases. The men had parcels containing gloves, handkerchiefs, and an elegant fob, and Adam had his neckcloths as well. The earl preened a bit over the cane topped with clouded-amber that he had acquired, showing it off to his fond wife with a trace of pride.

Emma stared at Adam Herbert as though she hadn't

seen him before. In his fine new coat, his highly polished boots below the biscuit breeches, and the intricately tied cravat, he was almost a stranger to her. Gone was the countryman; in his place stood an elegant gentleman, one who sped her pulse merely by smiling at her. She wondered if he would smile so for Amelia Jameson? She had never truly experienced jealousy before, but she had little trouble recognizing it as such. It did no good to berate herself for such foolishness. Why be jealous over a man you couldn't have?

Dinner was dispatched with just a bit of haste, with a promise to indulge in gooseberry pie upon their return from the evening's entertainment. They were at the theater in ample time to settle in their chairs prior to the play. Emma doubted if there was anyone more eager to enter the rented box than she was. Adam sat next to her, to her delight.

She had never been to the theater, so everything was new and fascinating to her. Looking about the interior, she took note of the three tiers of boxes, their crimson and gold decor now filling with splendidly garbed patrons. She noticed the box where Mr. Jameson sat with his sister while Sir George and Mr. Ives sat behind. Mrs. Jameson looked complacently on. And well she might, for they made a handsome group.

She thought it a shame her father so neglected her education, not to mention her entertainment. Surely with ample money at his disposal he might have seen to a season in Bath for her even if she hadn't gone to London? But she had observed over the years that while he was not slow to spend money on something he wanted, when it came to anyone else he had deep pockets and short arms.

"Is that not your cousin on the far side of the theater? There, below, near the entry door," Gussie whispered to

Emma when the others were occupied in arranging their cloaks and chairs or studying the playbill.

Emma cast a glance in the direction Gussie gestured. "It does appear to be him. I shall pretend I do not see him, then I shan't have to acknowledge him at all." She gave a little flounce in her chair, turning so her line of sight was nowhere near her cousin. She didn't fear criticism. Amongst strangers, few would know of the relationship.

Gussie frowned. "I do hope you can keep away from him."

"Rest assured I want nothing to do with Claude Polkinghorne!" Emma whispered furiously. "He seems to have a knack of getting me in trouble, no matter what I do or say."

It appeared that her cousin was not interested in her, for he didn't seek her out—or anyone else in the party. At least before the play began.

The first production was *Macbeth,* with a play called *Love for Love* to follow. The latter was a play that had been around for years but would be as fresh as newly written as far as Emma was concerned. Gussie reached out to touch her lightly on the arm, exchanging a smile of satisfaction at this treat.

The highlight of *Macbeth,* oddly enough, was the dance of the witches. Lady Stanwell explained that only in Bath did one see the performance of the ludicrous prancing around, which invariably brought the house down. Tonight was no exception. Enthusiastic applause came from the gallery as well as other parts of the theater.

Emma could not contain her giggles, nor could Gussie. A look of merriment exchanged with Adam Herbert caused the most peculiar sensation within

Emma. It was a bubbling up, a pure joy shared with a man one admired.

He leaned forward to whisper, "I see you enjoy the nonsense. I doubt this is done in London."

"Her ladyship said it is only done here. Pity, that, for it does take away some of the grimness." She gave him an apologetic grin. "I cannot say I admire the characters in this play. Of course I have read it, but it is far more affecting to actually see the roles portrayed." She glanced at the stage again, then back to him. "I believe I shall enjoy the play that follows a little better."

At the intermission, Gussie and Emma were able to meet Amelia, Louisa, and Jane to exchange views on the silly dance performed by the witches.

"It made me shiver, for it seemed too frightful," Jane declared fervently.

Gussie nodded agreement, nudging Emma to take note of her hovering cousin in the background.

Emma grimaced back at her dearest friend. Claude might look the perfect gentleman, but they knew what a numskull he was.

"We had best return to our box," Gussie urged when she noticed that Claude seemed to be edging closer.

"Ladies," Adam Herbert said with an obliging smile, "allow me to walk with you. It may not be entirely safe for you to be without a male escort here."

Emma caught the swift appraisal he gave Claude and was thankful for the protection Adam offered. While she didn't think Claude actually meant her harm, he could be unpleasant. Still, he was her cousin and . . . maybe he would improve.

"Mr. Herbert!" Amelia Jameson cried in patent admiration. "How noble you are to maintain such a kind watch on us."

He had not, thought Emma, offered to escort those

three to their box. He had come to offer his protection to Gussie and her. His moment of indecision was eased by the arrival of Rawlinson. The viscount offered to walk with Amelia and her friends to their box, thus mitigating the problem for Adam. Emma wondered where Mr. Jameson, Sir George, and Mr. Ives were. Surely they could have danced attendance on the Jameson party?

She was utterly horrid, Emma decided. She had no right to prevent Adam Herbert from becoming better acquainted with Amelia Jameson, and she took herself to task for her selfishness. For all she knew, Amelia had a splendid dowry that would enable Adam to have his heart's desire, the neat estate in the country where he could practice his farming methods.

She was somewhat distracted through the remainder of the *Macbeth* production. The acting was likely fine; she had too much on her mind. Was there any way that Adam Herbert might be made agreeable to her father as a son-in-law? Not that he showed any inclination to achieve that state, she admitted dryly. Her fascination with him was just that, and the interest appeared all on her side.

Before she knew it, the first play ended and they rose to parade in the foyer prior to the next offering.

"Did you enjoy your first taste of Shakespeare, Emma?" Rawlinson asked.

"Well, I venture to say it was well done. Of course, I know nothing of drama, so I am scarce qualified to judge. The dance was comical."

"I think it was vastly amusing," Amelia said, beaming a coy smile up at Adam from a beguiling face.

Emma gave his arm a faint tug, reminding him that it was time for them to return to the box. It was not, she mentally insisted, because she wanted to end the flirtation between him and the delicious Amelia. She didn't want to miss any of the coming play. *Love for Love* sounded intriguing. A comedy seemed a perfect antidote for the gloom engendered by *Macbeth*. Although she had not had the pleasure of reading the comedy, the author Cosgrove was well known.

The play was enjoyable, the comedy not too broad, yet truly funny.

They were well into the play when there was a stir behind as the door to the box opened and an usher brought in a folded note that was directed to Emma. She gave the bit of paper a puzzled look. For the oddest reason, she felt it to be something unpleasant.

She unfolded the note handed to her to learn that her cousin had important news for her about her father. He wrote he had been trying to tell her earlier but had been kept from her side by the attentions of the others.

Her first thought was that something had happened to her father. He and Claude were reasonably close, and if the news was dire, perhaps it was deemed preferable that Claude break it to her. Fearful for her father's health, she decided she had best meet Claude. She would go alone, not wishing to have anyone miss the delightful play. She had been overly suspicious about her cousin. He had only wanted to give her news from home.

Rising from her chair she shook her head at Adam when he half rose from his seat, indicating he was willing to go with her. Waving aside other offers of assistance, she slipped from the box, looking about her with puzzlement. She began to walk toward the front of the theater and the stairs to the ground floor. Her cream taffeta gown rustled quietly as she hesitantly made her way, wondering what news Claude had for her. He had wished to speak with her alone, and that made her uneasy. Still, they were in the theater, amidst a huge number of people in spite of the lateness of the season. Perhaps there were many who dreaded the darkened theater for the month of August when no plays were offered.

At last, near the bottom of the stairs, she spotted her cousin standing off to one side. "What is it, Claude?"

"Come with me," he insisted. "You must go home at once." He reached out for her, firmly taking hold of her arm.

She immediately resisted his clasp, pulling away from him. "Claude, I'll not go with you until you fully explain yourself and just *why* I ought to go home now. Surely it could wait until morning. I have no desire to travel at night, nor do I think it safe." She trembled with alarm.

"But it's your father! He's taken ill!" Claude tugged at her arm again, and again she resisted, pulling free once more.

"Why do I not believe you, Claude? You have that same look on your face you always wear when you are lying." With that, she wrenched her arm from his hold and ran away from him. Circling around the back of the theater while frequently glancing behind her, she kept running. Her slippered feet made little sound on the wooden floor.

He was gaining on her. What a pity she didn't have the dainty gun father had ordered made for her in her new reticule. That would stop Claude! "Leave me alone, you dastard!"

A man left his box. Emma would have sought help, but she doubted she would be believed. In her experience, a man would accept the word of another. She had no doubt Claude would make perfect sense to a stranger, one who had no knowledge of his duplicity. She ran on.

A wall with a plain door in it loomed up before her. What on earth could she do? She should have sought the box in the opposite direction where the Stanwells and others sat instead of this foolish dash. Why couldn't she think ahead to see the pitfalls before her rather than acting first and thinking later?

Claude reached out to grasp her arm again.

"You will come with me, dear cousin. I'll not have you tumbling into the arms of another, especially Adam Herbert! I can't abide that man! You will come away with me. I have your father's blessing. We can be in Scotland before you know it and then you and all that money will be mine."

"You are mad!" she whispered, her voice a mere rasping sound. There was no choice for her. She slipped past the door to find herself in a bewildering area full of background flats and people rushing silently about, while only feet away from her the actors and actresses portrayed the characters in the comedy. It had to be funny, for laughter erupted from the audience. Emma wished she were safely back in her seat. Why, oh, why had she thought her cousin might actually be honest for once!

Then he was behind her.

Her cousin—looking insufferably smug—blocked her path around the rear of the stage. She panicked. With a sob, she dashed onto the stage. Claude would not dare follow her there, as obsessed with his reputation as he was. Perhaps if she made an utter fool of herself he would be so horrified he would henceforth ignore her. Of course, that depended on how badly dipped he might be.

The audience tittered at the entrance of one not on the playbill. Emma gave the nearest actor an appealing look. "Please, save me," she whispered. She took a few hesitant steps, wishing the floor would open up so she might simply vanish. Of all the madcap things she'd done, this topped the list.

"Ah, fair lady, methinks you have the wrong play!"

The audience laughed. Emma wished she could die.

The chap calmly took her by the hand and marched her off the stage to the opposite side. They were followed by a gale of laughter when one of the actors made an amusing remark about how pretty women never seemed to be available when he wanted one.

"Where must you go? I gather you are running from someone." He smelled of greasepaint and sweat. As far as she was concerned, it was as nice as bay rum. He had rescued her from a dire plight.

Impressed at his perception, she gave him the number of the box where the others sat, and he pulled her along with him until they stood before the door.

"I trust things work out for you, but I suggest you avoid the theater for a time." He gave her a cynical look, then spun around to rush back to the stage.

If Claude lurked in the distance, she didn't take the time to check. Emma slipped inside the box, then threaded her way past the others to her chair.

Adam Herbert leaned over, his worried look touching her heart. "What happened? Claude?"

"Indeed," she whispered. Claude had done it again, made her look like a fool. She ought to have known better than to think for a moment that he truly had a message from her father. Had she not tried to cope on her own—not wishing to have any of the others miss a moment of the comedy—she would have had the protection of a man. Adam had bested Claude. Why had she not permitted him to escort her to where Claude waited to play his nasty little trick? She definitely qualified as a want-wit.

The comedy must have been amusing. Everyone, save Emma, laughed often. She was so wound up in her misery she heard not a word. She had really done it this time, gone beyond the pale.

At last the curtain went down and they could leave. The countess gently took Emma by the hand, drawing her along with her before anyone else could manage questions.

"What happened, my dear?"

Tears glistened on her lashes, making it difficult for Emma to see. "Claude . . . need I say more?"

"As a matter of fact, yes. What did he want that compelled you to leave the safety of our box? And how in the world did you land on the stage?"

"At first he told me my father was ill and needed me. But actually Claude wanted to abduct me to Scotland. He thinks to compel me to marry him. He must be badly dipped to try such a ruse. In fleeing from him, I ran the wrong way and . . . ended up in the middle of the first act!" She suspected her attempt at nonchalance was not successful.

She accepted the handkerchief someone offered her to blot her tears. It was hard to compose her nerves, but she would *not* put on a raree-show for others. She tilted up her face and attempted a smile, quite as though the entire episode had been planned.

Amelia Jameson and the others soon thronged about her, asking questions, the girls looking shocked. Amelia clung to Adam Herbert like a leech, looking demure as a nun. She would never get herself into such a pickle. Emma fought against more tears, bravely smiling and urgently drawing her little group to the nearest exit.

"It was merely a joke," Adam explained to the others.

Emma was thankful for the silent return to the White

Hart. Once in the sitting room, a full explanation was sought.

"Well," the countess declared once silence again reigned in the room, "we must attend the assembly tomorrow evening and prove nothing is amiss as far as we are concerned. As Adam said earlier—it was a joke." She nodded in regal finality.

Emma closed her eyes in humiliation and thanks for good friends. Just when she thought life couldn't get much worse, she was faced with braving the censorious society of the assembly rooms. She turned aside, longing for her bed and soft pillow into which she might silently sob.

"I ought to have insisted on going with you," Adam said in a low voice. "I know what Polkinghorne is like. You are too trusting. I fear your cousin is *not* a nice person."

That was the understatement of the year!

Chapter Twelve

When the party had left the theater, the countess had smiled serenely at several people she knew, including Lady Tate and her party. No hint was given that anything was even slightly amiss.

However, at the White Hart Emma was not granted the release she wished. They sat for some time discussing the plays and Emma's dramatic appearance on the stage. She felt she deserved a scolding. It was almost worse to have them all commiserate with her.

Adam Herbert joined her, gently placing his hand on her shoulder. He could feel her tremble, she was certain. She had been too alarmed to react while on the stage; now she felt all the panic return. It was hard to say which was worse—the time on the stage or the threat of being abducted by Claude for a dash to the border.

She had never been so humiliated. "It was like my worst nightmare come true," Emma admitted. She gave them a wary look. On her other side Gussie reached over to pat her hand.

"Actually, I wonder if anyone in the audience realized you were not a part of the comedy," Adam said. "The other actors covered for your sudden appearance very well." He hoped his words might allay her fears, but he suspected that those for whom gossip was their life-blood would subject her to tattle.

"We shall know tomorrow evening when we attend the assembly . . . assuming, of course, that I will be permitted to enter those hallowed premises." She spoke with the slight bitterness of one who has endured unjust scolds far too often.

"Actually, you might not have been recognized by most," he said. "Few people in Bath know you. We have been here a short time, and most of that has been spent shopping. I shouldn't worry too much if I were you." He patted the hand so trustingly placed on his arm.

Adam wanted to put a protective arm about the young woman at his side. She was impulsive, but he didn't think she was deliberately the madcap that Rawlinson called her. Casting his gaze down at her taut face revealed clearly in the light of the Argand lamp, he thought she looked terribly vulnerable. She needed someone to watch over her and keep her from tumbling into disasters. Perhaps if she had someone to give her loving care, she would cease her occasional impetuous behavior.

Most of the time, she was all that a man could wish in a wife. And actually, were her infrequent starts all that bad? She could scarce be blamed for this latest caper. Claude Polkinghorne was at the root of her problems from all Adam had observed. He recalled the first time he had seen Emma, she had been at Polkinghorne's mercy then. The situation had *not* been of her doing—even if she attempted to cover for him and insisted she could manage, it was clear she could not.

He realized that he would very much like to have the right to protect her from all ills, particularly Polkinghorne. What a cousin for a lovely young woman to have! Anyone, for that matter. And what a pickle for Adam—to want so much to take this lovely woman into his care and not have the means to do so.

Rawlinson had hinted that she was quite well off financially, which made matters all the worse. Adam would not wish to be thought a fortune hunter. While an ample dowry might make it possible for him to purchase a small estate, he'd not wish to do it through her money. Was he too proud? He suspected his friends would tell him he was a fool to pass up a chance to better his lot in life.

He knew a longing to draw Emma close, comfort her with kisses and a good deal more. What utter nonsense, he scolded himself. She would probably hit him over the head with her reticule. And rightly so, for no gently bred woman should be subject to such whims. Only it wasn't a whim on his part.

Miss Emma Lawrence was becoming an obsession with him.

"Tomorrow will determine how things will go," the countess observed, pouring herself another cup of tea. "Actually, we might be making a mountain out of a molehill." She sounded hopeful.

Rawlinson had considered the matter for a time before he spoke. "Cheer up. The tabbies of Bath would not dare to offend the earl and countess . . . or me, for that matter. I have observed that at present, peers are a bit thin of the ground in Bath. They may gossip, but that is all. Perhaps they will wonder if you went on stage as a wager, or if it was a part of the play . . . in which case, you may be looked at askance. They take a rather dim view of actresses," he concluded thoughtfully.

"Either one of your options leaves me in a bad spot. I should think I am condemned no matter what." Emma spoke with a bit more spirit, giving Adam hope that she would not fall into a severe case of the green melancholy. A woman of lesser spirit would have had mild hysterics by this point. Emma merely tilted her chin, ready to do battle.

Adam lightly squeezed her shoulder. "You have friends who will stick by you."

Algernon, Sir George, and Mr. Ives knocked at the door, then came into the room. They chattered about the surprising turn in the second play when Emma had suddenly appeared onstage. Apparently the gossip had even now begun, for they offered what little they had heard.

"Daring thing to do, I must say," Algernon Jameson said with a nod. "I'd not have the courage to face an audience of that size. Any size for that matter."

"Miss Lawrence was placed in an extremely awkward position," Adam said in her defense. "Her cousin is to blame for her stage appearance. It would be best to spread about the idea that it was just a joke. It is a shame when a young woman isn't safe from her own cousin's attentions. She wants no part of the fellow, yet he persists. Had she not dashed onto the stage I daresay he might have compelled her to fly with him to Gretna Green! He's that sort of chap."

The horrified men, now ignoring Emma completely, discussed what might be done to mitigate the effect of her moments on the stage of the Theater Royal. Over a glass of the earl's claret they agreed that something ought to be done about Polkinghorne, but couldn't decide precisely just what would be best.

Emma was all for booting him from the country since murder was not an option.

"Nasty piece of goods, that fellow," Jameson declared.

Adam wondered what, if anything, might be done to send Claude from Bath. Judging by the expression on

Emma's face, she thought Claude deserved the worst, whatever that might be.

"Think there will be a problem at the assembly tomorrow evening?" Sir George inquired with a worried frown, glancing at Lady Stanwell. Miss Lawrence was universally admired by the gentlemen as being a good 'un, but they all knew the whims of society gossips.

"I should think that if we all take her under our wing, solicit dances, and make it clear that we do not hold that momentary lapse against her, all will be well," Rawlinson said, patting Emma on the back. "I've known her forever, and there isn't an improper bone in her body."

"I think," Emma offered in a small, tight voice, "that I would like to return to my home."

"Can't do that," Mr. Ives insisted, sounding troubled. "You must show those country tabbies that you are innocent. Shouldn't be hard to do if we take you up," he added in all due modesty.

"With all of you at my side, perhaps I might prevail. I'll not give up yet." Emma gave each of the gentlemen a trustful smile, earning a look of support from each, even Rawlinson.

"Precisely what happened?" Mr. Ives asked. "All we know is that Claude was somehow involved."

"He must have acquired so many debts that he is become quite desperate! He wants to flee to Gretna with me, compel me to marry him—the lily-livered villain!" Emma left her chair to stand near the fireplace, wanting to take the chill from her heart.

"He is a horrible creature! Well," the countess declared, "we must take great care that you are guarded at all times. Claude must not be permitted to get his hands on your fortune. That your father can tolerate that disgusting fellow is more than I can understand."

"Perhaps he wants to keep the money and control in the hands of a family member?" Sir George mused.

"It would not remain there long if Claude had his way," Emma said, her voice tight from unshed tears. "He would gamble it away in no time and I would be left with nothing."

Adam looked from the earl to the countess. Had he heard right? He knew she had some money. But a fortune? Or were they making it sound like that when it was a more modest sum? Either way, it made things more impossible for him. He might adore her, but he'd not propose marriage to an heiress!

Gussie poured a cup of tea for her friend, then offered one to Adam. He declined, rather accepting a glass of claret from the earl. Rawlinson crossed the room, pouring a glass as well.

"Well, I believe that if the gowns we ordered are not ready by Friday we shall have them sent on to us. Tomorrow we shall visit the Sydney Gardens early on, then in the evening attend the assembly. Is there anything else you would like to do?" Lady Stanwell looked at the young women with a speculative gaze. "More shopping?"

"I intend to brave Milsom Street in the morning. There are one or two little things I need to purchase." Emma looked at Gussie, who nodded.

"I will go along with you in that event," Adam insisted. "Claude just might rise before noon, and I don't think Gussie would be much help in fending him off."

Rawlinson chimed in at that point. "I'll join you. If there are four of us, how could anyone attempt anything untoward?"

Emma blushed a delightful pink. "That is most kind of you—all of you," she said. That she looked only at Adam Herbert was not lost on the countess.

That dear lady frowned, contemplating what had to be done. She shooed the girls off to bed, soon following them.

Their new friends clattered from the room with Adam and Rawlinson in their wake.

Emma was greatly comforted by their support. It remained to be seen if Amelia Jameson and her friends would stand by her. They hardly knew her. It would not be unreasonable if they decided to avoid association with someone who had committed such a scandalous indiscretion. Before she had turned more than a few times, she was soundly asleep.

The rose-sprigged muslin was delivered about the time she prepared to dress, so she happily put it on. Perhaps with a new gown, and such a pretty one, she could face the day with optimism. She left the inn with Adam, Gussie, and Rawlinson at her side. Of the odious Claude there was no sign.

"I will not succumb to *any* of his ploys again, you may be certain," Emma declared. "Lady Stanwell said I am too naive. I don't think so. Rather, I was concerned about Papa. He does not take care of himself as he ought. When Claude said he had urgent news from my father, I was immediately concerned."

The others nodded in understanding.

Emma bought a pound of fine Hyson tea to take home, and then they all walked to the Sydney Gardens. There they found the other gentlemen waiting. To Emma's delight, Amelia, Louisa, and Jane were with them.

Emma exchanged a smile of relief with Gussie. They were ten in number. Just let Claude attempt to touch her now!

"Tell us what *really* happened," Amelia begged.

Raising her brows in dismay, Emma obliged, with reluctance. As briefly as possible she related how Claude had lured her from the box with the promise of a message from her father. "He implied it was dire news. I should have suspected him of villainous motives. How I could be so foolish as to think he actually meant kindly! I won't be caught out again, I promise!" What she did not reveal is that she had tucked the little pistol Papa had given her in the depths of her reticule. Men tended to take such a dim view of any woman attempting to handle a firearm of any kind, but she was trained.

"It shows your tender heart," Amelia said, her kindness evident in her manner. "You worried about your father."

"However, we have begun spreading the word that it was all a joke," Adam said.

The topic was dropped in favor of the lovely day, the ball at the assembly that evening, and what each planned to wear.

Emma, never having been to the Vauxhall Gardens in London, was entranced from the moment they entered. The hotel at the entry was quite splendid. Rawlinson promised they should partake of tea there later. He left them a few moments to bespeak the treat. Gussie went with him. They returned together in a brief time, both looking quite pleased.

"Pity we don't have our horses," Algernon Jameson said with a lingering look at the ride that surrounded the garden. "Rather nice, that."

Emma glanced in the same direction, taking note of the stylish ladies and gentlemen riding along the broad path. She also took note that Claude was not among them. But, as Rawlinson said, Claude was not one likely to rise early.

"There are pavilions, bridges, lawns, groves, waterfalls, and vistas," Amelia said with delight. "I was here before, and they are truly admirable."

They sauntered along the main path of the gardens, enjoying the morning, pausing now and again to peruse some statue or amusement. The labyrinth was ignored.

"We had best not go in there. It would be too simple a matter for Polkinghorne to lurk about in the hopes of luring you off to something or other," Rawlinson decided.

"You must think I am an utter peagoose to be taken in by that man again." Emma glared at the gentleman who had teased her unmercifully from early childhood, not that she had seen that much of him. What she had seen had been quite enough!

They strolled through the Gardens from one end to the other, enjoying the waterfalls and the grotto of antique appearance. The shady groves offered a pleasant retreat from the summer sun. They admired the Merlin swing but were not inclined to have a go at it.

"It would be nice to see the fireworks once," Gussie said with a sigh. "I hope I can come here again someday."

"Perhaps we could forego the assembly this evening to take it in?" Amelia ventured.

"You may do whatever you please," Emma said dryly. "Lady Stanwell insists I must attend the assembly tonight and so I will. Although, I confess I should like you all there with me."

That ended any discussion about fireworks or missing the assembly. Rawlinson wore a thoughtful expression on his handsome face while he watched Gussie when she staunchly defended her friend. She insisted they would all be there.

Back at the hotel they enjoyed a sumptuous tea in one of the small alcoves that gave onto the garden.

From this spot they could see all who entered and left the gardens.

Really, Emma thought, Rawlinson was being very amiable. Fancy recalling how much she enjoyed toasted teacakes.

By the time they returned to the White Hart, Claude had receded to the back of everyone's mind. It was a pleasant day, and the evening promised to be all they could wish.

The countess had definite ideas on just how Emma must look that evening. The lavender India mull had been delivered, lavender ribands must be threaded through her hair, and her pretty gold locket was to be her only adornment.

"We want you to look elegant, but not pretentious," the countess declared, eyeing the lavender reticule and white gloves that were to be worn. She added a delicate sandalwood fan.

Emma wasn't certain just how elegant she might look, but conceded that the India mull was very fine indeed.

By the time they had dined early—during which Emma could scarcely eat a bite—and left for the Assembly Rooms, she was in a mild panic.

The younger men clustered about her chair, intent on protecting her from danger . . . and Claude. Adam walked the closest. He might not be eligible to marry her, but he could jolly well act as her defender. The men stopped under the portico to allow her to exit the sedan chair.

She gazed at the doors with trepidation. How she wished she might be anywhere but here this evening. Well, not anywhere. She wouldn't want to be making the mad dash to Scotland with Claude!

First taking a deep breath, she left the shelter of the

chair, accepted Adam's arm, and then walked to the entry.

Rawlinson and Sir George opened the doors for them. And finally she was inside, traversing the interior corridor where a number of people were lined up, probably waiting for friends or family. Emma wondered if anyone was curious about her. Then she mentally shook herself for believing for a moment that she warranted that much attention. The earl and countess were before her, so naturally attention was focused on them!

The ballroom was to their left, and they entered it through the antechamber. Emma lifted her chin, not really looking at anyone in particular. She sensed there were eyes fixed on her, but hoped they were kindly.

The Master of Ceremonies bowed to the countess and the earl, then beamed a smile at Rawlinson. No doubt he was delighted to see such distinction grace the rooms this evening. If he had heard a word about Emma's scandal of the night before it certainly wasn't revealed in any way. Perhaps being in the party of the esteemed Earl and Countess of Stanwell—such highly regarded members of the *ton*—made the difference? It couldn't hurt that Rawlinson was at her side. That Gussie was on his arm made little difference, they were all together. After all, Adam Herbert was the earl's great-nephew, and that was nothing to sneeze at either. Introductions were extremely formal and the earl was at his most forbidding—gruff and starchy.

His performance was awe-inspiring to anyone who didn't know him well. Had Emma not known him as far back as she could remember, she would have been most intimidated.

They made a regal procession across the room, the Master of Ceremonies, a Mr. King, Rawlinson said, graciously bowing them to favored seats. Lady Tate bowed from where she perched on a chair. Admiring looks were seen on many of the faces turned their direction. Mr. King appeared excessively pleased.

Emma took a deep breath and pressed Adam's arm with her fingertips. "It seems that word of the unexpected actress in the play last evening has not reached *his* ears at any rate."

Rawlinson leaned over to softly add, "Even if it had, you are in exalted company. King would not dare turn his nose up at someone who has the approval of my grandparents."

The orchestra played the introduction for the first set, a stately minuet. Since Emma and Gussie hadn't learned the steps, they were more than content to sit quietly, enjoy the music, and eye the other occupants of the room with care.

Rawlinson strolled about the room, looking handsome and restless. He motioned for Adam to join him.

"Do you see who just entered the ballroom? None other than the despised Claude! Since these are public rooms he cannot be denied. Also, it is known that he aspires to Emma's hand, thus making him the future possessor of considerable wealth."

"Just how much wealth are we talking about here," Adam asked, his curiosity demanding to be satisfied.

"The last I heard she is to have an income of somewhere around five thousand a year. Upon her father's death I should imagine the estate would be valued at fifty thousand, possibly more. You can see why the devious Claude wants to marry her." Rawlinson crossed his arms before him, then tapped his chin as he considered the newcomer.

"He will not be allowed a dance with Emma," Adam declared firmly, putting aside this new knowledge. "It is too simple for him to dance her over to the entry, then spirit her out the door before any of us have a chance to act. And to post one of us at the entry would seem strange to others."

"True, true," Rawlinson agreed. "It requires the utmost vigilance. We shall have to be creative."

"The other chaps know to be on their guard. I don't suppose they perform the waltz here? It is danced in London, I hear. My sisters all learned to waltz. It would be easier to keep her away from Claude's clutches with a waltz. But somehow I have the feeling that life is a bit more reserved in Bath."

Rawlinson chuckled. "That, my cousin, is putting it mildly." Ignoring Claude, who had begun to walk toward them, the two men made their way back to Emma and Gussie.

"Claude has come," Rawlinson said abruptly, not cushioning his words. "Never fear, we shall not permit him to get near you." He cast a scowl at the toad who threatened his friend.

"What is to say that he doesn't join the same set?" Gussie inquired, patting Emma's hand in a reassuring manner.

"Simple, my dear Gussie. We shall take care to form our own set—always. There are ten of us, and that makes it quite possible, don't you think? I'll have a word with Mr. King."

Adam watched his cousin approach the Master of Ceremonies for a brief conference. When he returned he wore a satisfied smile. "I expect that will take care of everything."

The following dance was a longways country dance. The group hurriedly formed a set. Emma faced Adam, Gussie, his cousin.

Lady Tate and her party nodded in apparent approval that so attractive a group of young people, all known to one another and with the distinguished earl and countess, took the floor. Benign smiles bloomed among the dowagers and chaperons.

Emma thought she had never had such a delightful time in her life. After all the worry and fretting, it was so wonderful to relax and to enjoy the pattern of the dance. True, Amelia Jameson flirted with Adam Herbert when possible. Gussie twinkled a smile up at the dashing Rawlinson. The others went along charmingly.

Claude stood off to one side, grimly watching.

After casting him a look of loathing, Emma turned her back on him, intent upon the dance. By the final steps, they were all eager for a glass of lemonade—at least the young ladies were. The gentlemen might wish for something else, though it was unlikely they would get it.

Claude had the temerity to approach the group as they sipped their drinks and eagerly discussed the other attendees in the assembly rooms, the fine dance just concluded, and what they might do on the morrow.

Rawlinson held up his polished quizzing glass to stare through it at the encroaching Claude. The effect was so utterly devastating that he paled and left the assembly rooms at once.

"Well, he has fled the field. We may relax and enjoy the rest of the evening," Adam said with huge satisfaction—which they proceeded to do with engaging enthusiasm.

Chapter Thirteen

Lady Tate came to call the next day following nuncheon. She arrived with several friends in tow, three mousy little creatures with scarcely a word to offer.

"My dear Lady Stanwell, how charmingly you looked last eve. And the young people with you! Well, I doubt Bath has seen a more delightful group in simply ages. The young ladies were certainly a credit to you. Even after that odd appearance of Miss Lawrence on the stage, she captured all eyes and hearts." There was a question in Lady Tate's voice and manner. She perched, expectant, and looking like an owl hunting for prey.

"Dear Emma feared she was sunk beneath reproach, but truly, she didn't know what to do with her cousin opportuning her, and she not wishing to be whisked off to Gretna."

Lady Tate's cool gray eyes narrowed. "Claude Polkinghorne, I gather. I went to school with his mother and a greater peagoose I have yet to see. It is no wonder he is as he is. And his father is the greatest nodcock on earth, thinking he can win back his fortune by playing cards when all the world and his wife know what a dreadful card player he is."

Lady Stanwell nodded in agreement. "Which is, of course, why he pursues his cousin. Poor child! Fortunately, she has made some splendid friends while here in Bath. I had thought to suggest that her father permit her to attend school here. But with Claude lurking behind every tree, that wouldn't be wise."

"The best thing would be for her to marry. How blessed she is to have a fortune. She can wed where she pleases." The ladies with Lady Tate nodded eagerly.

"Not always," the countess replied prudently.

Lady Tate shot the countess a judicious look. She nodded ever so slightly. "How fortunate she has you to assist her."

The countess let this pass without comment. "You took note of my grandson and great-nephew last evening, I trust? I believe my grandson will make a match of it before long. I won't mention any name, for that might spoil the scheme. But I am pleased."

"How nice," Lady Tate replied, clearly wishing she knew more, but knowing she dare not inquire.

"This is our first visit with our great-nephew. He's such a fine young man. Pity he has no fortune, but with five sisters and our nephew but a rector, there was little chance of it. You know how it can be in the church."

"I heard the daughters married well."

This gave Lady Stanwell the opportunity of revealing precisely just how well those "poor" darlings had done.

That the callers were impressed with thoughts of a marquess, an earl, a baron, a baronet, plus Lord Nicholas—the brother of the marquess—was clear. It was a collection of titles any mother might be in alt over. Lady Stanwell was clearly pleased.

Emma happened to enter the room at this point, only to find herself the focus of every eye.

"Ma'am? Is there anything you wish when we go

out? Gussie and Rawlinson, Mr. Herbert and I, plus all the others plan a ride into the country around Bath."

The countess exchanged a look with Lady Tate. "As long as your escorts can keep you safe, my dear."

Emma smiled, quite neglecting to inform Lady Stanwell of the neat little pistol nestled in the reticule dangling from her arm. It was carefully placed so as not to be noticed, tucked in the folds of Emma's pretty rose-sprigged muslin. "I shall be fine, dear ma'am. Mr. and Mrs. Jameson go with us as chaperons. Sir George thought it wise." She studied the countess to see what her reaction might be.

After praising the Jamesons as most amiable people, the countess said, "I decided we will remain in Bath until our gowns are ready. The earl agrees with me. So, if anything requires adjustment, we will be where it can readily be done." The countess gave Emma a cautioning look.

Emma took it as a warning to be on her guard against her crafty cousin. She gave a firm nod of her head before offering the callers her best curtsy and slipping from the sitting room.

"Well," Lady Tate mused, "she's not rag-mannered. But with her fortune she may be anything she pleases and only the highest of high-sticklers will object. And who gives a pin what they have to say about anything?"

The countess nodded graciously while pouring tea for her callers. If she wished things a trifle calmer, it wasn't revealed. Anyone who knew the countess well would know she was having a marvelous time.

In the hallway, Gussie and Emma each took a deep breath before marching down the stairs, parasols and reticules in hand.

"Did you tell her where we will be?" Gussie asked.

"I informed her that we intend to venture into the

countryside," Emma replied. "With our impressive contingent, we all should be protected against wild beasts and importunate nuisances. I'm glad the Jamesons consented to go with us. Algernon Jameson said his father is a crack shot."

"I do not see how you can joke about such matters. Claude is desperate. Sir George learned that he has plunged further into debt while here in Bath! I hope the man I marry is not a gamester." She gave a dramatic shudder.

"Well," Emma said carefully, "Rawlinson does gamble a bit, but no more than he can afford. I should think he would be inclined to put that aside once married—responsibilities and all that. Even if we battled as children, I do like him."

Gussie gave her an alarmed look.

"Not enough to wish to marry him, however." She knew that Gussie's parents would welcome Rawlinson with open arms. What intelligent parent would turn up a nose at a handsome viscount due to inherit a vast and profitable estate—not to forget the earldom? The Dunlops were most intelligent parents!

They had reached the bottom of the stairs, where Adam Herbert awaited them. Emma beamed a smile at him, wishing he were not unacceptable to her father, as he was sure to be no matter how many peers his sisters had married. The mere sight of him sent her heart into a flutter.

A line of carriages had drawn up on Stall Street before the inn. Adam helped Gussie into the elegant cabriolet belonging to the viscount, who today looked quite splendid as he held the reins to his fine horse. His polished style of dress set him far above the others. Yet he was most agreeable, and that was what counted, Emma decided. The viscount deigned to greet Emma, a smile in his eyes.

"Morning, Emma. Ready for everything?"

Emma narrowed her eyes and wondered if he guessed what she had in her reticule.

"I am certain I shall enjoy every moment of our charming excursion. After all, what could possibly happen when I am so well guarded?" She dipped a slight curtsy and grinned, twirling her parasol with her free hand. The other kept her deadly bundle safely from view.

Jane Mytton and Sir George rode in the third carriage, with Algernon Jameson and Mr. Ives escorting Amelia and Louisa in a respectable landau. Adam assisted Emma into the phaeton the earl had arranged for him to use.

Mr. and Mrs. Jameson drove in a very neat cabriolet, not unlike the one Adam Herbert owned.

"We shall be quite a parade!" Gussie cried as Rawlinson led off the group. Adam was second in line.

"Note that there is one vehicle in front of us and three behind. There is no way that Claude will be able to come near you while we are enjoying our outing."

"Where are we going? Or is it to be a surprise?"

Adam grinned. "Rawlinson thought you might enjoy a glimpse of Wells, the cathedral in particular."

Emma thought he possessed a rather endearing grin. "That should be very nice. I would like viewing a large church. It is a pity you decided not to go into the ministry."

"Well, as I said before, there is a dearth of openings. Until some fellow dies or actually retires, there is little chance of gaining a vicarage. Besides, what I really want to do is manage an estate. I like the challenge of growing things. I managed my father's affairs for some time.

He tends to be absorbed in his writing—religious articles, you know. Since I can't afford an estate of my own, I'll accept the earl's offer to study under his steward."

"That sounds a sensible plan," admitted Emma. The knowledge that he would be close by pleased her. If Claude became even more persistent—although it was hard to imagine how he might—she could perhaps call on Mr. Herbert for help.

Adam followed Rawlinson at a discreet pace, admiring the scenery and once in a while glancing at the tempting young woman at his side. He could do no more than look, what with the others immediately behind them. Still, she was an eyeful. Her perfectly shaped oval face with the straight little nose and flawless skin; the pretty mouth that smiled far more than pouted. Quite exquisite! He knew a pang of regret that she could not be his chosen mate. Still, he would do all he could to protect her from Polkinghorne, dastardly chap that he was. It seemed to Adam that keeping the money in the family was a poor excuse for a marriage.

The distance to Wells from Bath was about twenty miles, give or take a few. It was such a beautiful day, he truly didn't care if it took a long time to get there, but they made good time.

He followed Rawlinson into the heart of the town, right to the Market Place and the courtyard of the Crown Inn. Here they left the carriages. Adam was impressed that the inn had the staff to take the influx of carriages with nary a blink of an eye. According to Mrs. Jameson, they also possessed a splendid private parlor where the group might refresh themselves before viewing the cathedral. Naturally they decided upon tea first.

"You will want to see the famous clock, I daresay," Algernon declared to Gussie and Emma. "'Tis one thing I truly enjoy seeing. Every quarter hour those knights come out and before they retreat manage to beat one knight down. Quite diverting." For Algernon it was a long speech, and he was faintly pink when he finished.

"I am certain it will be delightful," Gussie replied with a smile. She sat by Rawlinson. He seemed very solicitous of her.

Amelia came up to the little table where Emma, Adam, Gussie, and Rawlinson sat with their tea. She gave Adam a teasing regard. "We shall all go through the cathedral together. I shall welcome a strong arm to assist me. Those aisles are so rough. Last time I was here I stumbled, and had it not been for my gallant escort, I am sure I'd have fallen."

Vincent Ives gave her a knowing look, tucked her arm next to him, and said, "In that event, allow me to play the gallant."

Emma almost laughed at Amelia's look of disappointment. While it was understandable that she found Adam Herbert to her taste, she would do better not to make it quite so obvious. Emma was pleased that Adam did not give Amelia any encouragement. He was utterly proper in his behavior . . . to all the young women, more's the pity.

When they left the Crown Inn the group didn't stay closely together. Louisa spotted a shop that had precisely the sort of gloves she had been wanting. She and the obliging Algernon, with Amelia and Sir George as well, entered the shop and were lost to view. The elder Jamesons followed the others.

Emma wondered if she could become accustomed to the close watch that she had endured on this trip. But then she realized it was for her own good and relaxed some, thankful that she had someone like Adam Herbert as her escort.

Gussie exclaimed over the swans that were so clever

they knew how to summon bits of food twice a day by ringing the gatehouse bell. She and Rawlinson dawdled by the moat, watching the dignified birds so gracefully gliding along the water.

Not wishing to intrude on the lingering couple, Adam and Emma continued on to the cathedral. Since there was not the slightest evidence that Claude had followed them on the outing, Emma felt safe enough to stroll into the magnificent building. She suspected that Adam wished to inspect the interior of this famous cathedral in some detail. She was perfectly willing to dally with him.

They were relatively alone, not that they would consider the faintest action that might be deemed improper! For one thing, you never knew who might stroll around a corner, and there were a great many of those. They had entered by the great west door and proceeded to where they could examine the splendid font.

"It looks to be exceedingly old," Emma observed, stumbling on the paving. She felt a delicious warmth when Adam clasped her arm to steady her. Really, she was being absurd to react so strongly his slightest touch.

After admiring the unusual font, with its crownlike cover, they continued along that side of the building to peek into St. Katherine's chapel, after which they looked at the lectern and other small chapels at that far end behind the high altar.

"Do you think your father might ever serve as a bishop?" Emma wondered.

Adam smiled at her, that bone-melting smile that affected her so much. "I doubt it. He is not one to enter into politics. And, even if the earl might put forth his name, it is doubtful that his influence, while considerable, would be sufficient."

"I haven't met your father, but I don't doubt he deserves the position." Emma accepted his arm. She needed support.

"There are many fine clerics eligible for the post if it became vacant. My sisters would have it that the earl could see to the appointment. I am the one who is more realistic."

She made no reply to this. They admired the beautiful stained glass windows, their footsteps echoing in the silence. Voices reached them from a seemingly great distance, resounding through the vastness of the cathedral interior.

"I imagine the others have finally joined us in exploring this lovely place," Emma said after a searching look behind them. She heard people speaking but could not see them.

When they reached the area opposite to where the font stood, they found the enormous clock that was tucked into a recess in the north transept.

"I must say that it is rather difficult to decipher the correct time," Emma declared after a study of the immense timepiece.

"According to the paper we took as we entered, it was made in 1390. At every quarter hour the figures of the armed knights pop out and one of them, as Algernon said, gets beaten down. That's a twenty-four-hour dial. The larger star is the hour hand and the smaller star acts as the minute hand. I must say I agree—it isn't the simplest clock I have ever tried to read." Adam looked at the slip of paper in his hand, then back at the clock, shaking his head.

Footsteps alerted them to the arrival of another of their party.

"Perhaps one of the others will have a good notion of how to decipher it," Emma said dubiously.

They both turned away from the picturesque clock to

discover who had caught up with them. They were shocked. It was Claude, a most unwelcome addition to the group.

"I had no idea that one of the grotesque figures on the walls might come to life. Unfortunately, they are depicted with humor and you are never that. Good day to you, Claude. How did you know we had come to Wells?" Emma demanded to know, her heart accelerating rapidly. She associated Claude with disaster.

"If you think that a cavalcade such as you were part of could assemble then go south from Bath unremarked, think again. A question or two and I learned it all."

"What do you want with us? For I assume you did not join us merely to praise this cathedral." Emma gave him a scornful scrutiny. She noticed that he held his arm in a rather odd position. For some reason this bothered her enough so that she carefully brought her reticule up even with her waist. She pretended to hunt for a handkerchief after remarking to Adam that she thought she had a speck of something in her eye.

She also dug her elbow into Adam's side, hoping to alert him to potential danger . . . if that was necessary.

Offering that nasty little grimace that passed for a smile when Claude thought he had the upper hand, he stepped from the shadows of the pillar separating the north transept from the aisle leading to the chapter house. The reason for the odd position of his arm was disclosed when he raised his hand to reveal a nasty little pistol he had concealed.

Emma delved to the bottom of her reticule to close her fingers over her own pistol. She couldn't imagine what it would be like to fire it inside a building like this, but if it was necessary, she would. She was more determined than ever not to be forced into marrying her stupid cousin. That he persisted in his pursuit indicated to her his desperation.

"Turn around and walk to the north porch entrance. Go outside there," Claude instructed in a soft voice.

"Well, I am glad that you have no intention of shooting one of us inside this cathedral," Emma said in a dry voice. "Heaven only knows what would happen."

"Silence," Claude snapped quietly. "I don't want your friends to hear us."

"Worried your disgusting behavior would be caught out?"

"Polkinghorne, this won't get you anywhere, you know," Adam said in a reassuringly firm voice.

Emma began to slowly withdraw her little pistol, hoping that Claude would be so preoccupied in steering them where he wished them to go that he'd not notice her actions. She had turned as directed and walked with great care to the north porch. Glancing around she noted that not one of their party was in sight, although she could faintly hear voices from the far side of the interior.

"Don't think of uttering a word, cousin," Claude warned. "I am willing to shoot inside, even though I'd prefer to be out of doors. I have you where I can spirit you away quite easily. If you value Mr. Herbert at all, you will be docile for once and obey me—and your father, I might add."

"Oh, pooh," Emma said, not bothering to lower her voice in spite of her cousin's cautioning. "You cannot make me marry you, try as you will."

"I venture to disagree. I can and I will." He waved them ahead into the porch, then out onto the green beyond.

With her back turned to her cousin, she withdrew her hand, the gun at the ready.

Adam sharply drew in his breath. He stepped closer to her, to Emma's relief. Surely Claude would not shoot Adam when he was so close to her? Claude was not the best shot in the country. But then, neither was she. She did not wish to kill anyone, even her wicked cousin. Could she manage to shoot him and merely wing his right arm, thus preventing him from using the weapon in his hand? Was she that good a shot? What if she killed him?

She gave Adam a panicked glance. "Oh, help!" she whispered, hoping he would understand her problem.

"Do not think you can protect your fancied gentleman, dear cuz. Had he not paid you such noticeable attentions, he would be in no danger today." Claude motioned them forward.

"I do not understand why you worry about Mr. Herbert. He does not seek my hand. Even if he did, what makes you think my father would welcome him as a suitable husband for me? Why Papa thinks *you* worthy is beyond my understanding!" She discreetly maneuvered so that Adam could take the pistol, not trusting herself to be accurate if push came to shove.

"Move away from him!" Claude demanded, his voice rising even higher than its usual tenor pitch.

Emma felt faint with relief when Adam slipped the gun from her hold.

"I suggest you drop your pistol, Polkinghorne," Adam said, a note of steel in his voice.

Claude snorted in disdain. "I think not!" He leveled his pistol at Adam, sneering in confidence that he had the upper hand over Adam as well as his cousin.

From behind Emma, Adam whipped out her pistol, aimed, and shot before Claude could realize what was happening.

A thin trickle of blood dripped down Claude's

sleeve. He dropped his pistol, staring at his arm and the blood in obvious disbelief. The sudden flash of pain had shocked him so he had no thought of firing his gun. He clutched his arm, stunned.

Rawlinson dashed from the north porch to join them. "I don't need to ask what is going on here. Polkinghorne, do you never learn?"

Emma sank back against the reassuring strength of Adam Herbert. "When it came to it, I couldn't shoot him. I wanted to, but I thought I might actually kill him. I am not so good a shot that I trusted myself," she explained in a troubled voice.

Rawlinson left Emma to Adam's tender care, striding across to where Claude still stood in utter incredulity. "Come, you do not deserve the least pity, but I'd not have you distressing the ladies in our party." To Adam and Emma he added, "I know where there is a physician. I'll turn Claude over to his attentions."

Emma watched her cousin leave with Rawlinson. "I can't help but wonder what he will try next."

"Next? You believe he will not cease his attempts?" Adam asked.

"Indeed. I am convinced there is no good in my cousin." She turned away from the sight of Claude disappearing with Rawlinson at his elbow. "Let us return to the cathedral interior. Poor Gussie will wonder what has happened."

Gussie lurked just inside the door to the north porch. "I have never been so frightened. Will he never stop? I think someone ought to lock him up until you are married, Emma."

Emma gave Adam a swift glance. "That might be nice but probably not possible. Do you believe my father would accept what has happened without argument? Besides, I have no plans to wed at the moment. It could be a long stay for Claude."

"And I say good riddance to the man," Gussie retorted.

There was no quibbling with this sentiment. The three returned to the interior of the cathedral, walking slowly as the shock washed over Emma. Her white face drew anxious looks from her friends.

"I am fine. No need to treat me like fragile porcelain." Emma, however, gratefully accepted Adam's arm. The danger that had imperiled Adam had struck her when she watched him pick up the deadly little pistol where Claude had dropped it.

The Jamesons bustled up to Emma and Adam. "What has happened? We heard a shot outside!"

"It was just my cousin, ma'am," Emma said dryly.

"He is here?" Mrs. Jameson cried in alarm.

"Rawlinson has escorted him to a physician. He was shot."

Mrs. Jameson fainted.

Chapter Fourteen

When Mrs. Jameson had fully recovered from the shock of learning that Claude had been winged in his attempt to spirit Emma away to Gretna, the group decided to start back to Bath following a light nuncheon. No one, it seemed, wished to remain in Wells, all interest in the cathedral quite faded away.

"I am exceedingly tired of Claude, I must say," Emma mused over a bit of pork pie at the Crown Inn. "Although I'd not wish to see anyone dead, it is a pity that you merely winged that obnoxious, stupid idiot."

"Emma!" Gussie cried in horrified accents. "That is a highly improper thought." Her fork clattered on her plate as she stared at her dearest friend as though she were a madwoman.

"I know," Emma agreed placidly. "But then, you are not the one who is having to tolerate his repeated proposals and attempts at kidnapping. I daresay there is not a worse abductor in the kingdom. Not that I wish him to improve, mind you. At the moment, I can think of nothing worse than being wed to him!"

"Well," a slightly mollified Gussie answered, "I can see what you mean about that. But what are we to do?"

Rawlinson gave them an amused stare. "I have arranged for someone to look after Claude until he can be transported back to Bath. I'm sure not one of us wishes to be saddled with him."

"You have the right of that!" Emma said at once. "His parents have a deal to answer for. What about his horse?"

"Taken care of, my dear." Observing that everyone seemed to have finished their meal, he continued, "Now, I shall put Gussie in my carriage, Herbert will assist Emma into his, the others will follow suit, and we shall be on our way."

"Lady Stanwell will not be pleased to learn our outing was spoiled by my odious cousin," Emma told Adam quietly once he was up beside her in the cabriolet.

"There must be some way we can impress upon him the necessity of leaving you alone short of arresting him." He skillfully tooled the vehicle from the yard of the Crown Inn, following Rawlinson out of the pretty little town.

"If my betrothal was announced, he might turn his attention to some other heiress." Emma sighed, knowing the futility of that, as any parent of sense who had an heiress would be most careful to keep a daughter out of the way of a fortune hunter. Pity her own father had no sense, at least when it came to his nephew. And there was no other prospect in sight for her.

Once in Bath they all went their separate ways. Gussie and Emma, with Mr. Herbert and Rawlinson at their sides, trudged up the stairs to the sitting room. Any hope that the countess might be elsewhere was dashed upon opening the door.

"You have returned rather early, I must say. What went wrong?" The countess looked from one to the next, her expectant silence demanding a reply.

Adam put a supporting arm about Emma's shoulder. "Claude showed up."

"What happened?" the countess asked with a hint of iron in her voice. "I can see he didn't make off with Emma."

"He would have done so, ma'am. Mr. Herbert shot him, just grazing his arm as a warning. I must say, it was effective. Claude dropped his gun at once. He was quite stunned." Emma gave Adam a proud look. "Mr. Herbert is a hero."

"Tell me, Adam, do you always carry a pistol when you intend to visit a cathedral?" the earl inquired from the doorway to his bedroom.

"Actually, the gun was mine," Emma confessed before Adam nobly accepted the guilt. "I am mistrustful of my cousin. So . . . I decided it was sensible to be prepared for anything, for I now admit that Claude is quite capable of being nasty."

"I truly do not think him to be very bright," Gussie added.

Rawlinson grinned at that. "I arranged for a physician to look after him and someone to tend to his needs. Beyond that, I did not think necessary. He will likely turn up here before we know it. After all, it was the merest graze."

The earl nodded, studying Emma where she stood in the protection of Adam Herbert's arm. "I say we should head home the day after tomorrow. Claude will still be in Wells, most likely."

Emma turned to look at the earl. "How well you know him, sir. He will malinger in bed, enjoying being waited upon. Not that his mother does not pamper him at home," she added scrupulously. "It is a pity he is their only child."

Gussie sniffed. "The others might be worse."

Adam handed Emma's gun to the earl, who had imperiously held out his hand for it. "Here you are, sir."

"Well, if Claude is abed in Wells, I ought not need it," Emma decided, looking rather thoughtful. "On the other hand, one never knows about thieves. What if we are held up?"

"I had no idea what a bloodthirsty girl you are," Adam said, with a polite smile for the earl after glancing at her.

No one was in the mood for going out that evening, so they stayed at the inn, playing silly games and laughing a great deal. If the shadow of Claude's behavior lingered about, no one actually spoke of him. He scarce deserved any sympathy.

Later on, before retiring for the evening and after Rawlinson and Adam Herbert had left the sitting room, Lady Stanwell studied Emma for a few moments.

"I do not know what your father intends to do with you, my dear. You must know it is imperative that you marry. Your father seeks to wed you to his sister's son. I believe it would be an excellent notion were you to find someone else before your father puts his foot down."

"True," Emma admitted. The last thing in the world that she wished was to be joined in matrimony to her rotten cousin. Everyone knew how she felt. Even Claude knew how she felt, although he didn't permit it to deter him in his pursuit.

"We shall have this party with the Jameson youngsters and their friends, culminating in the ball. I hope that while they are staying with us you will be able to fix your interest on one of the gentlemen. They are all eligible, you know."

"So I understand," Emma said. She felt no attraction to Algernon Jameson, Sir George, or Vincent Ives. Actually, she suspected that Sir George was more than a little taken with Amelia, while Algernon always partnered the pretty Louisa. Mr. Ives and Jane Mytton might not be enamored of one another, but unless you attended the matrimonial bazaar during the London Season, you had to make do with whatever came your way.

That she far preferred Adam Herbert was left unsaid. She suspected that even the countess, who vastly deplored Claude, would look askance at her interest in the earl's great-nephew. He had no prospects as far as Emma knew. She couldn't understand why she simply couldn't offer him her dowry and the lavish income she enjoyed. True, her father would have spasms! That thought brought forth a wry smile of satisfaction.

"Well, we shall see how things go," she temporized. She would not promise anything. If you didn't make promises, you didn't have to worry about breaking them.

Two days later the earl and countess led Emma and Mr. Herbert, Gussie and Rawlinson out to where their carriages waited for them. Adam and Rawlinson climbed into the viscount's cabriolet while Emma and Gussie joined the earl and countess in their traveling carriage.

Boxes of gowns purchased in Bath plus all the other items that had to be brought back to Stanwell House were neatly stowed in the extra carriage brought to carry Lady Stanwell's personal maid, his lordship's valet, and Rawlinson's valet. It was a good thing that Gussie and Emma had been more than willing to do for each other while in Bath.

Emma supposed that as an heiress she ought to have insisted upon her own maid, but it seemed to her that since the Stanwells were paying the bills, it would be a bit much for Emma to impose another maid just for herself. She was sadly lacking in *ton*, she supposed. She certainly had little vanity.

The trip home was spent discussing their purchases and the many interesting shops, the theater—with no mention of Emma's disastrous debut on the stage of the Theater Royale—and the assembly they had attended. When this topic of conversation was exhausted, the countess retreated into a nap, as did the earl shortly after.

An overnight at Beckhampton Inn proved insipid. Absolutely nothing dangerous happened. The earl had returned her pistol to her just before leaving, and Emma thought it rather splendid of him. Of course it was unloaded. She fixed that at first chance, much to Gussie's dismay.

"There is little point in carrying a pistol if it is not loaded. I am sure no robber would pay me the slightest heed were I to threaten him with it empty of shot." Emma gave her dearest friend a patient glance, then loaded the nicely cleaned pistol with an expertise that might have given the earl pause had he been aware of it.

"I was sorry to leave Amelia, Jane, and Louisa. And Sir George, Mr. Jameson, and Mr. Ives as well," Emma added, seeking to be fair. Just because she had not the slightest interest in the gentlemen didn't mean she considered them unworthy. Most likely they would pair off as she expected they would. "It will be nice to see them again at the party."

"It will be jolly to have ten young people around," Gussie said wistfully. "I liked being in Bath. There is so much to do and so many people to see. Why, you could go out every day and not see the same people twice."

Emma gave her a skeptical look but didn't have the

heart to point out that if one were there very long the same people would be there as well. She had learned that most of the people who came to Bath would stay on for several weeks, if not months. True, there were new names in the Subscription Book at the Pump Room every day, but most stayed on and on.

The *Bath Herald* published the names of those being married. Emma had no wish to have her name included on that list—together with the amount of her fortune. It amazed her to see people felt a need to know such personal details. Fancy reading that Emma Lawrence would be married, along with the information that her dowry was so many pounds, with grand expectations!

By the time the carriages rolled through Peetbridge they all were worn to a nub and only too willing to step from the vehicles. The servants immediately set about removing the parcels and baggage while the travelers went ahead.

When they entered the house, Newton at once gave Emma a message from her father. She thanked the butler, read it, and then gave the countess a distressed look. Rather than explain, she simply handed the little missive to the countess.

"Good grief! Your father is staying in Salisbury for an indefinite time. Whatever . . .?" She turned to her husband, handing him the brief note that revealed precious little.

If the earl had his own notion of what his neighbor might be about, he said nothing regarding it. "You shall stay here with us. Claude might not be home yet, but you never know when he will pop up like a bad penny."

"I should be more than happy to assist with preparations for the coming party, ma'am," Emma assured the countess. "I would like you to tell me what you wish, and I shall do as much as possible." Emma figured that if the earl and his dear wife were going to the lengths of having a party here, it behooved her to do all she could to help, even if the party was to introduce their great-nephew and honor the heir.

Gussie reluctantly departed for her home, her parcels and gowns adding considerably to her baggage.

Offering her good friend a warm hug, Emma whispered, "You will come back here to help me, won't you?"

Gussie lost her forlorn expression. "Indeed, I will."

"We will plan a few outings for the Jamesons and the others, something special."

Gussie gave her friend a cautious smile.

"I know what you think, but I will not disgrace us. I promise to be on my very best behavior."

Gussie looked rather alarmed at that bit of comfort. Her friend at her best was only slightly less dangerous than when on an adventure.

"Go, then. We can talk later on," Emma promised.

Putting aside her curiosity regarding her father and what he might be doing in Salisbury, Emma instructed Nancy regarding which parcels were hers, then joined Lady Stanwell in the drawing room.

Newton brought a tidy pile of mail to the countess.

Emma sank down on a mercifully unmoving chair. Why was it that the constant motion of the carriage hadn't bothered her on the way to Bath, whereas coming home was exceedingly tedious!

She studied the countess where she sat looking over her mail. What could she do to assist this kind lady? She soon found out. She was to arrange flowers, and meet with the housekeeper and the French cook, Alphonse, to plan menus the young people would enjoy. Alphonse was a most temperamental man and had to be gently persuaded in the right direction.

She headed for her bed with her head awhirl with all that had to be done. The following day she began first thing.

Emma wrote out invitations in her best hand, taking note of all the local people who were invited. The ball would be beyond anything she could recall. How Gussie would adore it, particularly if Rawlinson intended to seek her hand. Their forthcoming marriage might even be announced at the ball!

The thought of marriage put a momentary damper on Emma's spirits. But she took heart, determined to thwart her father at every possible turn.

The housekeeper took careful note of who was to attend the party and whether or not the parents would be present. Room was needed for maids and valets on the top floor of the house. Newton would see that the proper wines were available, although it would be unusual for the earl's cellar to be lacking.

Emma checked the floor plan, observing who was to be placed where. It seemed fine to her. The girls and their families were to be in the east wing while the gentlemen were in the west. How fortunate that a gentleman did not require his family to chaperon him! True, not all fathers would attend, but she would wager most of them would. The Earl of Stanwell had not entertained for simply ages. This was a party no one would wish to miss. Rawlinson and the earl would design entertainment for the gentlemen. The countess would oversee activities for the ladies. Emma intended to see to her contemporaries.

While the Stanwells were in Bath, the footmen had lowered the ballroom chandeliers for cleaning, and now they glittered in the morning sun, awaiting the lighting of hundreds of candles.

"I believe it best if Gussie stays here with us for the

party. She will miss a great deal if she must return home each day," the countess decided, tapping a letter against her chin.

Emma checked the plan of the house, and finding a room still empty, penciled Gussie's name on it.

The following days were filled with preparations. Emma was in her element, dashing upstairs to check on the room for the Jamesons—there had to be two beds—then back to the kitchen to tell the pastry cook about Amelia's love for cinnamon buns. The gardener was warned that Emma would raid the beds for flowers. John Gardener nursed his prime vegetables for Alphonse, only nodding when informed of her intent.

Of Adam, Emma saw very little at all. He had gone off with Mr. Chambers, the steward, immediately following an early breakfast. He was present at meals, sitting next to the earl to discuss what he had learned and offering some of the latest opinions on land management that he had read about in recently published books and periodicals. The earl listened, and on his other side, Mr. Chambers nodded, agreeing with much of what Adam said, offering a counter thought where he differed.

It was clear to Emma that Adam Herbert thoroughly loved the work, the planning. From the morning room window she watched him stride across the stable yard, a hat sitting jauntily on his head, his crop in hand, intent upon what he was learning. Although, according to Mr. Chambers, Adam had the head knowledge, he merely needed the opportunity to put it all into practice. Printed information was all well and good; a man needed to see if it proved practical. Emma hoped the earl was as impressed as she was.

Yet she sorely missed Adam. She had become accustomed to having him at her side while in Bath, coming to her aid so many times. He might remain at Stanwell, assisting Mr. Chambers, with whom he got along very well. That fact didn't mean she would be able to see him, spend time with him again. An heiress was not supposed to mingle with—much less admire—one of the help.

"He is doing well, I understand," the countess said from over Emma's shoulder. "My husband is pleased with Adam and the progress he shows."

Emma half turned to take note of the expression on her ladyship's face. "It would seem so. He will be glad to remain here with you and study with Mr. Chambers. I trust the earl will be able to nudge Adam, that is, Mr. Herbert, to a good position." She thought a moment before adding, "My father would have a seizure if he thought I was interested in Adam—someone who actually works for a living."

"Yet your father works very hard. True, he breeds horses. But he does well. And, in the end, is raising a horse that much different from raising a crop?"

Emma said dryly, "Try explaining that to Papa."

"Do not overlook the matter that Adam is my husband's great-nephew. That places him far above a mere employee. Just you wait. I feel it will all work out for the best."

Emma longed to ask "work out" for whom? She kept her tongue between her teeth and made a wish.

At last the day came when the guests were scheduled to arrive. The Jamesons came first. Algernon handed Amelia from the carriage with brotherly regard, that is to say, not a great deal. Mr. and Mrs. Jameson glanced about them, looking a bit awed at the vastness of Stanwell House when they entered the grandiose hall. Newton favored the foursome with a wintry look. The first footman motioned a lower footman to escort the valet and abigail upstairs to their rooms.

Mrs. Fancourt and Louisa had joined forces with Mrs. Mytton and Jane in a carriage, with their gentlemen riding outside. They bustled inside, the older ladies darting glances about the sumptuous entry while the girls eagerly sought Emma and Gussie, exclaiming over the house and the fun they would have.

Emma looked out the window to spot Mr. Ives and Sir George in a fine curricle coming up the avenue that lead to the main house, pulled by a splendid pair of chestnuts.

Rawlinson joined Algernon to greet their friends. Algernon entered the house, giving the entry an admiring look. "This is something like," he murmured to Rawlinson.

Sir George also looked around, turning to Rawlinson to add, "Where is Herbert? Surely he hasn't left?"

Rawlinson grinned, shaking his head. "This time of day he will be out with the steward. He takes his new position of assistant steward seriously."

Of course this had to be explained, and they greeted this news with a mixed reaction.

Amelia sidled up to her dear friend Louisa. "Poor Emma, she must be quite devastated. Think you that Claude will win after all?"

Louisa gave her bosom friend a cautioning look. "Never," she whispered in return. "She would run away first."

The group gathered in the spacious drawing room. Amelia immediately spotted the harp sitting near the far windows. "Promise you will play for us later, Emma!"

"She does rather well at the harp," Rawlinson drawled as he sauntered in behind them.

"The earl enjoys having me play for him, so likely I will later on," Emma promised.

"And will we see Mr. Herbert?" Jane inquired, one brow lifted just a trifle.

"I believe he will join us come evening." At least Emma hoped he would, if he wasn't too tired. Yet he appeared to revel in being out in the open, striding along with Mr. Chambers as though he owned the earth.

Once everyone had been escorted to their various rooms and freshened from their drive, they all returned to the main floor where tea was to be served to the ladies. The men preferred the claret and sherry offered. They spoke of the roads and their difficulties in getting to Stanwell. The ladies talked of the coming ball, hinting that there might possibly be interesting news to share. During a party at a country great house, many hearts could be joined. And every mother present had high hopes for her precious girl.

The countess leaned back in her favorite chair to inspect her guests. Rawlinson was with Gussie, quite as she anticipated. When the pretty Louisa entered the room, Algernon made his way to her side, chatting with an easy familiarity. Hmm, the countess thought. They appeared to be on a comfortable footing.

His sister Amelia gave Sir George a shy smile when she came into the room, thus crossing him off the possible list. When Mr. Vincent came in together with Jane Mytton, the countess was most disheartened. It seemed to her that they were all paired off like so many animals of the ark.

It remained for her to do something about Adam Herbert. One would have to be deaf and blind not to see that Emma was top over toes in love with the young man. He needed money—which Emma had in abundance, if only he would accept a wealthy wife.

He wasn't like Claude, for certain. Adam had scruples, and above all, the earl genuinely liked him. She cast her mind about to see what solution might be found. It would take some managing, perhaps even a bit of prodding, but she believed she might find a way—if some nodcock didn't do something stupid.

They drifted off to their rooms, the various parents to enter into serious discussion as to the prospects of their children. The air seemed to hum with speculation when they returned downstairs after the sound of the dinner gong.

Adam obeyed the summons to dine. After the attentions of Rawlinson's valet, he looked quite as impressive as any of the other young men.

The countess watched her husband beam with pride at his two young relatives, and her hopes rose. She had always done well with her adroitness in guiding her dear husband. It ought not be too difficult when he was half inclined that way to begin.

After dinner, Emma gathered the younger group about her. "Since the weather has turned so nice, I thought it would be vastly agreeable to take a picnic along to the Kennet and Avon canal tomorrow. There are pretty walks and ample wildflowers." The girls nodded eagerly, while the gentleman looked wise.

The Jamesons dampened schemes by volunteering to chaperon.

Chapter Fifteen

The weather cooperated the following morning with warm sunshine and few clouds. Even the breeze was gentle.

The only shadow on Emma's horizon was the knowledge that Adam would not be with them. He was to accompany the steward on some mission for the earl.

It had been impressed on her mind that with her heart given to Mr. Herbert, it would be next to impossible to look in any other direction. Thus she became an efficient organizer for the day's entertainment, hiding her own disappointment well.

By ten the carriage awaited the ladies who wanted to keep their pretty dresses just so. The gentlemen all elected to ride. A vehicle loaded with everything needed for a picnic had gone on ahead to prepare for them.

Emma entered the landau with Gussie, Amelia, Louisa, and Jane. The carriage normally held four, but with such slim young women, it easily contained them all, parasols and bonnets notwithstanding. The Jamesons followed in the cabriolet.

The closest section of the Kennet and Avon canal was a bit north of the small town of Pewsey. When they reached the spot that the earl had suggested, the carriage drew to a halt close to a wooded area.

The men had ridden on ahead, so they had their horses tethered and were waiting to assist the young ladies from the landau. It had taken a little over an hour to reach the pretty meadow, and they were all prepared to enjoy some refreshment.

Emma bustled about, instructing the footmen who attended them to pour ale and lemonade for the party. Summer wildflowers still bloomed. Patches of delicate blue meadow cranesbill, white campion, and small blue scabious brightened the area. Delicate blue harebells nodded their fragile heads, adding dots of blue to the pastureland. Emma thought Eden might have looked like this, tranquil and lovely. The meadow had a clean, fresh smell, quite unlike the environs of Bath prior to a needed rain.

Large rugs had been placed here and there, as Emma decided it would be delightful to rusticate without the usual tables and chairs, not to mention all the linen, china, and other things so many thought important even on a picnic. Alphonse had sent excellent sandwiches with savory fillings, pork pies, plus a selection of fruit and a variety of biscuits and little cakes.

"Shall we walk first before we eat our picnic?" Emma politely inquired of those who were close by. Algernon and Louisa had wandered off. He picked clusters of campion and harebells, handing them to the gentle Louisa to admire.

"Walk first, eat after," Sir George declared.

Emma called to Algernon and Louisa to join the rest, and the group straggled along, pausing to admire a pretty sort of woods, stopping to listen to a birdsong, before at last reaching the canal. Louisa and Jane were tired and plopped down, albeit gracefully, on the grassy bank above the canal. Jane pulled a long stem of grass and twiddled with her fingers.

A barge loaded with coal slipped silently past, the bargeman keeping a careful watch on the boy who led the horse along the towpath. The horse plodded along and the boy whistled a merry tune, his stick in hand in the event he needed to remind the horse he had a job to do.

"They would have come down the sixteen Caen Hill locks this side of Devizes," Algernon instructed the pretty Louisa.

She fluttered her lashes over china-blue eyes and smiled. Her charming bouquet of campion and harebells added to her innocent beauty. Louisa was one of those who believed in silence to capture a man's interest. She listened with rapt intent, which seemed to please Algernon.

Emma was glad that Amelia had apparently given up on attracting Adam Herbert. She walked along at the side of Sir George, offering comments on the bucolic scene.

They sauntered along the edge of the canal, admiring a family of swans, their little ones still sporting the soft, grayish-brown feathers even though they were a fair size by now.

Emma had the forethought to have equipment for various games brought along. She carried rackets for battledore with her as well as the shuttlecocks. As they were lightweight and no trouble at all, she now brought them forth. "Who wants to play?"

Algernon and Louisa tried their skills first. When they tired, Sir George and Amelia attempted the game, but Amelia had not the least luck in sending the little shuttlecock soaring back to where Sir George stood patiently waiting. Jane declared it too warm to play a game, so Mr. Ives joined her on the rug in the shade of a tall tree to simply admire the day and talk about the amusements they enjoyed while in Bath.

Since the picnic was simple and quite easily moved, and no one seemed inclined to walk the short distance back to the original site, Emma asked the footman if the repast could be moved to the canal. Since they had the benefit of a wagon pulled along by a sturdy horse, it made little difference to the servants. The Jamesons retired to the shade of a tree.

Amelia and Sir George settled under a fine oak to sample the nuncheon set forth.

Trying not to be bored—for, after all, the picnic was her idea—Emma wandered along the edge of the canal, a sandwich in hand. She wondered what Adam Herbert was doing now, what occupied his time that was so important and necessary to the earl. She truly missed him. She missed his genial smile, his merry eyes when he grinned at her. She remembered his strong arms as they had wrapped about her slim form when that dastardly Claude was trying to abduct her from Wells.

"What are you thinking about?" Gussie inquired as she and Rawlinson joined Emma by the canal. "You look a million miles away."

"Nothing important," Emma prevaricated. How could she admit her thoughts were full of Adam Herbert?

"Tell you what, Em," Rawlinson said, "I'll go a few rounds with you in battledore. I wager I can beat you to flinders."

Emma tossed the remainder of her bread to the swans, then found the rackets and the shuttlecocks. She was doing rather splendidly, not missing a one of the serves that Rawlinson so ably shot at her, when she thought she spied Adam Herbert coming around the curve in the path.

Could it actually be him? Belatedly she hit at the shuttlecock, only to lose her balance while attempting to reach a high shot. She had run backwards to hit the dratted thing. In losing her balance, she tottered on the edge of the canal and with a scream to frighten every bird within a mile, she plunged into the water.

Adam had watched the rustic scene with pleasure. He had begged off the last duty of the day, joining the others with the earl's blessing. When Adam saw Emma teetering on the bank above the edge of the canal, he began to run. He knew Emma by now: If anyone were to have a disaster, it would be her.

As he ran he tore off his coat, then pulled off his boots at the edge of the canal before diving into the water that had been churned up by the coal barge passing so recently.

She sputtered as she surfaced, spitting out water. She pushed her hair out of her eyes, turning to Adam with a resigned expression on her face.

"I cannot believe I did that."

"I can. Emma, you need a keeper." She looked so woeful at his words he wished them unsaid.

"I was startled, you know."

"I can imagine. The last person you expected to see was me coming along the path." Adam managed to slip an arm around her slim body. He gently propelled them both to the edge of the canal, where Rawlinson knelt to assist them from the water.

Gussie stood beside him, one of the light rugs in her hands. "Emma, how could you?"

"I lost my balance. Rawlinson sent me such a serve, and when I tried to return it, I landed here." She looked at the water in disgust. Mrs. Jameson fussed in the background.

"I think I distracted her," Adam said, a pronounced

twinkle in his gray eyes. "Rawlinson, you pull, I will try to help from this end."

Emma glared at Adam at the very thought he mentioned her "end," then accepted Rawlinson's hands. There wasn't much Adam could do, but he tried. Sir George and Algernon offered their help to Adam, and in minutes he joined Emma on the grassy bank. They stood dripping, thankful it was a warm summer's day with only a little wind and bright sun.

"Best wrap up well in spite of the sun," Gussie advised.

"Here's a bit of ale," Sir George said to Adam, while Amelia brought a glass of lemonade to Emma.

"You will want to wash the taste of the canal water from your mouth."

Emma glanced at Adam and knew she blushed. Before she was gently wrapped in a rug, he must have noticed her clothes were plastered to her, revealing far too much.

She promptly sat down, huddled in her rug, wondering what she had ever done in this life to deserve such occurrences. Why should such awful things happen whenever Adam was around?

True, she had tumbled into calamity in the past, but now it seemed to follow her like a plague!

A footman came running with several large linen napkins. Adam thankfully wiped his face and hands with one, then blotted as much water from his clothes as he might.

Emma took a linen napkin to do the same. Gussie rubbed her hair with another. "It's a blessing you have short hair," Gussie said as she tried to fluff up the hair as it dried. "And it is surprising that the water wasn't dirtier. Your hair hasn't suffered as much as I would have expected."

Emma couldn't imagine what she must look like after the plunge in the canal. Her pretty lavender India mull was likely dripping lavender-tinted water.

"Oh, bother," she exclaimed in disappointment. "Please go on with the picnic. Pay not the slightest attention to me." Then she recalled the very wet Adam Herbert. "However, you probably want to return to Stanwell."

"Not on your life," he responded lightly. "The sun will dry me quickly enough. I want to visit with you all and have one of those tempting sandwiches. Another bit of ale would not be amiss, either." He turned to the footman, who quickly offered him a mug of ale.

Emma knew that if she hadn't fallen madly in love with him before, she would have tumbled at that moment. He looked so boyish, a lock of his auburn hair on his forehead, a rueful grin on those firm lips. Had Claude fallen into the canal, he would have raised a ruckus and complained loudly and long. Adam made a joke of it and smiled at her in a most disarming manner.

Once he polished off the ale, he pulled on his boots and dry coat, looking far better than she did. His shirt had dried in the sun and faint breeze. He looked vibrant and manly, and a faint scent of bay rum from his slightly dampened skin teased her nose. His voice was rich, not the least affected by his ordeal. And if there was a man more appealing, she couldn't imagine what he might look like.

Emma sat quietly to one side, pretending that she didn't mind looking like a drowned cat. She had felt so safe in his arms; perhaps she might concentrate on that.

"Emma," Gussie said in a worried little voice, "do you think we ought to return now?"

"I am fine," Emma lied. "There is no reason to go

back now when we are all having a perfectly lovely time."

She told herself she truly didn't mind having them all look at her as though she was a bit strange.

"I believe your father has come home," Adam said, giving Emma a keen look. "As a matter of fact, I think I saw his carriage coming toward Stanwell just as I was leaving for here."

She sat up a bit straighter. "You did?" She tried to sound as though she was not unduly concerned. "I thought he was going to remain in Salisbury indefinitely."

"He was there an indefinite period," Rawlinson reminded. "He didn't say precisely how many days. You thought quite a few, and it isn't many at all."

Emma felt very uneasy, and it had nothing to do with being half wet with damp hair and her dress looking anyhow.

"Perhaps . . ." she began, then stopped. She had promised herself she would help the potential betrothals, and she would. Papa could wait until they all returned. She doubted his news was important anyway. He had likely been absorbed in a horse race or something on that order.

Before long Emma found that she was reasonably dry. The little rug had blotted much of the water from her dress; the sun and slight wind did the rest. She watched Adam Herbert as he chatted with Rawlinson about some problem that had popped up out on the home farm. He discussed the matter briefly, but not so long that it bordered on being tedious. After all, as the heir, Rawlinson should be interested.

Rawlinson, she noticed, listened respectfully to the ideas that Adam advanced. He had studied to advantage, Emma thought proudly. Not that it would make any difference to her father, for whom money and position should have prime importance. If she lived to be one hundred she would never understand her father!

"I believe it is time to go back," Gussie commented to Emma. "Louisa thinks she got a bit of sun on her face in spite of her parasol. Jane looks as though she would prefer to sit on a chair rather than that large stone she is perched on now. And Amelia is making me ill with batting her lashes at Sir George. Louisa has done quite enough of that with Algernon Jameson."

"You and Rawlinson have not spent time idly, I think," Emma teased.

Gussie blushed and shook her head. "We are entirely proper."

"So are the others, but I expect you have the right of it." She rose from her resting spot and went to the wagon to place her folded rug on it. In short order all the rugs and sporting equipment were stowed, as was the leftover food.

No one seemed in a rush to leave the idyllic meadow. Even Emma knew a fondness for it, in spite of her dreadful tumble into the canal. Adam had been understanding, even if he declared she needed a keeper. And he placated Mrs. Jameson just so.

He brought Emma her discarded parasol before mounting his horse to return to Stanwell. With a flurry of muslin skirts and parasols, the young women entered the landau with much laughter and no hurry. It had been a pleasant interlude for all. Matchmaker Emma thought the various pairs looked more in tune with one another. She was the odd one out.

The horses seemed inclined to dawdle, and the men rode alongside the carriage, laughing and joking with Louisa, Gussie, Amelia, and Jane. Only Emma remained detached, wondering why her father had returned and come to Stanwell House first thing. She hoped he would not insist upon her going home with him. The way matters stood, she nurtured little fondness for the place—not with Claude apt to pop up whenever he pleased.

When they reached Stanwell, the carriage drew to a halt before the front entrance. The gentlemen turned over their mounts to the grooms, who had hurried from the stables when the sounds of approaching horsemen and the carriage were heard.

Emma waited until the others left the landau. She slipped out and around the idling couples to whisk past them into the house and up the stairs before anyone realized the group had returned.

It was worse than she had expected. How mortifying to have been so bedraggled in front of so many, particularly Adam Herbert. Her maid hurried in to assist her with removing the now-sad lavender India mull.

"I believe I can restore this, miss," Nancy said eagerly. She tossed the mull on the bed, then helped Emma into the blue French-cambric dress. It was more suited to company, but Emma wished her father to see her at her best.

It was futile to wish she could have time to wash her hair. Her father would expect her to come down promptly. However, a study of her face in the mirror told her it wasn't too bad.

The maid made short work of brushing Emma's hair, curling the sides around a finger to hang down just so. "Very fetching, miss, if I do say so." She bobbed a curtsy, then sped off with the lavender mull over her arm.

Emma rose from the dressing table bench to pace back and forth a few times, gathering courage to face her father. Would he have heard a word about the various ills that had befallen her while on her trip to Bath?

Before, during, and after, that is. She didn't see how he could. So why was he here?

Finally, seeing the silliness of staying in her room while she wondered about his presence, she marched down the steps to the drawing room, where she supposed her father would await her.

Rather than deep in conversation with the earl, as she had supposed, there were four people seated around the tea table. An older woman joined the earl and countess and her father. Emma gave her a curious look before executing a polite curtsy. "Papa, it is good to see you again." She would be exceedingly polite, no matter what.

"Come, Emma, I have someone I wish you to meet."

Warily, Emma approached the sofa where her father and the stranger were seated. She stood, wondering what was to come.

"Emma, I have a surprise for you. Meet your new Mama." He turned to the lady at his side, and with an indulgent smile of the sort that Emma hadn't seen in some time, he said, "Viola, this is my Emma. I know you two will get along famously." He sat back with a smug smile, looking like a wizard who had performed a difficult trick.

The new Mrs. Lawrence offered her hand, which Emma took in hers, wondering if she should shake it or simply curtsy over it. She did both.

"She is a lovely gel, just as you said." Her answering smile at her new husband seemed genuine. Emma wondered if she had married her father because he held a vast fortune. He would be a neat plum for any woman. Then she chastised her skepticism. Her father was a fine gentleman. This Viola woman was lucky to latch on to him. And anyone less likely to resemble a shy viola, that miniature violet peeking forth from spring greenery,

Emma couldn't imagine. She looked about as delicate as a rock.

"You will be impressed with Viola's horsemanship, Emma," her father said, one hand on his knee and the other gathering up a hand of his new wife to hold gently.

"We met at a horse show near Salisbury," Viola explained. "I was so impressed by the horse Mr. Lawrence was showing that I insisted I had to meet the owner."

"We hit it off right away. She knows her horses, that is for certain."

Emma gave the pair a strained smile, nodding dutifully. At a gesture from the countess, Emma moved to join her on the other sofa, where the countess reclined in graceful splendor. Emma wondered what the countess thought of her new neighbor, the new Mrs. Lawrence.

Emma's mind was in a whirl. What would happen to her now? Would her stepmother abet her husband in pushing Emma to marry the disagreeable Claude? If she sought to please her husband, Viola could well make life miserable for Emma until she did as her father desired. She shut her eyes against such a painful possibility. Opening them, she turned to give the countess a silent plea for help.

"You will be pleased to know we are in the midst of a small party here," the countess revealed to her callers. "I wanted to acquaint a few people with our great-nephew, Adam Herbert, as well as the earl's heir, Viscount Rawlinson. Emma has been an enormous help to me. I do not know what I would do without her. Promise me you will let her remain here with us until after the coming ball!" She smiled in that persuasive manner she had. "Besides, Mrs. Lawrence will welcome a quiet time with her new husband and to settle in at

Brook Court. I am sure you will find Mrs. Turner most helpful in assisting you."

"I trust you will admire the stables," the earl added. "Lawrence has the best of men out there."

Mrs. Lawrence beamed a smile at the mention of the stables. "Indeed, my lord. They are in top condition. Mr. Lawrence not only has prime horseflesh, but bang-up stable hands."

Emma exchanged a guarded look with the countess. Bang-up? No true lady would use such slang. Unless, of course, she was horse-mad or racing-mad to the point where she aped Lady Lade, a woman even Emma had heard about. Letty Lade had, previous to her marriage to Sir John, been the mistress of "sixteen-string Jack," a notorious highwayman who was later hanged. Emma had heard that she used abominable language.

"Indeed, my dear. If I do say so myself, there are few stables better than mine." Mr. Lawrence looked at his bride with a fatuous expression that sent a frisson of unease through Emma.

Neatly folding her hands in her lap, Emma inquired, "You do not mind if I remain here, then, Papa?"

"I am certain that Mr. Lawrence is only too happy to see his girl enjoy herself," Viola replied on his behalf. "When the party is over, I mean to help your father see you wed to his nephew. Such a fine young man. I am sure you want to please your papa, dear Emma—if I may call you that?"

Emma inhaled sharply. Her father was quite capable of answering for himself. But she knew how he felt about Claude!

The Lawrences left not too long after this. Once Newton had escorted them to the main door, Emma turned to her good friend, the countess. "Oh, dear ma'am. What a coil this is!"

"It needn't be, you know. But I foresee trouble ahead for you. She means to fix you up with your cousin Claude. Instinct tells me that she will wish to ingratiate herself with your father. I can almost hear the wedding bells now."

The earl had listened to the women quietly voicing their fears. "We had best do something before it is too late."

"I have an idea," the countess began, then stopped.

Gussie and Amelia, followed by Louisa and Jane, came into the drawing room. Gussie had checked at the door, then seeing Mr. Lawrence had left, apparently felt safe to enter.

"Well, you just missed meeting my new stepmother." Emma met Gussie's astounded gaze with her own grim one.

Gussie quickly found a chair and plopped down with haste. "Your father has married? Is this not rather sudden? Who is she?" Gussie looked to the earl and countess, then back to Emma.

"She is now Viola, Mrs. Lawrence. I sense that Papa must have met her at the racetrack, for she is very much into horses. Where else does Papa go when near Salisbury?"

"Oh, my goodness," Gussie whispered, looking utterly aghast.

The earl frowned, then his brow cleared. "It is not so very bad, my dear Emma. I have seen her before. She is a wealthy woman and owns a fair stable herself. At least she didn't wed your father for his money."

Emma wasn't sure if that was good or bad.

Chapter Sixteen

The countess supervised everything from her comfortable chair in the drawing room, occasionally drifting out to the terrace to view the various games and innocent pastimes considered appropriate for young ladies. Gentlemen might do anything they pleased, but they joined in the harmless pursuits with goodwill. Blindman's buff and hunt the slipper were simple games for children, but played by adults they took on an intriguing spice.

All week Algernon Jameson had sought out Louisa, and Sir George continued his pursuit of the pretty Amelia. Jane Mytton and Mr. Ives good-naturedly played along with the others at whatever was on offer. Emma was odd man out.

She longed for Adam to be with them. She had made a point of rising early so she might see him at breakfast for a brief time. These were treasured moments, even if the earl entered to discuss the progress Adam had made. He seemed enormously pleased with the talks and with all Adam suggested. Emma was absurdly proud of the man she so admired, even if he made little attempt to seek her out. She caught his eye on occasion and an infinitely sweet yearning swept through her at the expression in those fine gray eyes. It was as though he longed to talk with her but dared not.

After nearly a week of charming diversions during which Emma managed to avoid tumbling into serious mishaps, the day of the ball arrived. Adam had not been present to distract her. He, she thought longingly, was striding about his business looking far too cheerful for her peace of mind.

Gussie and the other young ladies chattered to one another at the breakfast table, preferring company to having a roll and chocolate in their rooms. Hesitant discussions of gowns and jewelry brought forth their inner fears. Would their gown be proper and fetching? It was difficult to walk that fine line between acceptable and being labeled fast.

As the day wore on, the young ladies retired for an afternoon rest, insisted upon by their mothers with the thought that the ball demanded fresh, eager faces. Often the dancing went on until dawn. Who wanted to be caught yawning!

The dinner was to be splendid. Days before Emma had taken Lady Stanwell's suggestions to Alphonse, who had praised her ladyship's taste and proceeded to begin work on his culinary creations with the assistance of his two under-cooks.

The time to join the countess and the earl in the drawing room to greet the invited local guests soon came. Emma left her room with reluctance. She awaited the arrival of her father and new stepmother with dread. When they entered the drawing room, her heart sank. A sartorially stylish, if somewhat amazing, Claude was with them. The periwinkle coat under which he wore a puce waistcoat that had gold threads woven through it topped his yellow satin breeches. Very peacocky! Emma thought that had his cravat been any higher, it would have prevented his breathing. What a pity he had kept it as low as he had.

"Cousin Emma, delighted." Claude bowed as low over her hand as his stiff garments permitted.

She returned his awkward bow with a slight nod of her own, just enough to be proper. "Cousin Claude, what a surprise. I was unaware you had received an invitation." Her smile had a deadly quality that he totally failed to observe.

"Your father was certain it was an oversight. He insisted that as your future husband I ought to come." He smirked. It was a knowing look, full of malice and horrid anticipation.

"Whatever gave you the idea that I will marry you, *dear* cousin?" she replied softly, her own voice loaded with sarcasm.

He merely sneered and walked on, preening.

Emma knew the countess had overheard Claude's statement. Turning to her benefactress, she sent her a pleading look.

"I have all in train, dear Emma. Do not fear. I want you to enjoy yourself this evening," she ordered.

Emma glanced to where Adam stood dressed in well-bred taste. An auburn lock insisted upon falling over his patrician forehead in a charming way. He might not be of the peerage, but he had the countenance that had been handed down in the Stanwell family for ages. It combined his looks with that air of command. Rawlinson had it as well. Tonight the resemblance was obvious as he stood alongside his great-uncle and his cousin Rawlinson. There was no mistaking the family nose or the regal bearing.

Taking a deep breath, she faced the next people who came up to her and greeted them with the graciousness she had learned from the countess.

As soon as the modest assembly of guests were all in

the drawing room, Newton entered to announce that dinner was served.

It was evident that those gathered had an excellent grasp of precedence, for they drifted to their proper partner with little guidance from either the countess or Emma. She ignored her cousin and walked to stand by Adam. She had discussed it with the countess, who had agreed it would be quite proper.

Emma's new stepmother darted angry looks at Emma, but they failed to intimidate her. She would show *that woman* that she could not expect to control Emma!

Dinner was as excellent as one might wish and that all expected of the Earl of Stanwell's hospitality.

Emma took note of the seating arrangements. She happily sat at Adam Herbert's side, while Gussie had been placed next to Rawlinson. Oh, she hoped it was a good omen of what was to come.

Her clear broth had savory flavor and the fish course had a piquant taste that must please. She sampled a bit of roasted turkey and the beef collops with broccoli. During the pause that occurred between the first and second course, she chatted with Adam. He seemed a trifle remote, as though he felt a constraint. Either that or he had something on his mind. She hoped he didn't permit the glowering looks from Claude to bother him. She refused to allow Claude to disturb her pleasure in the evening.

Lobster ragout and lemon tart comprised her choice of the second course. Adam offered a sample of dressed woodcock and she accepted because she thought he wanted her to taste them.

"You are fond of woodcock, Mr. Herbert?"

"Tolerably. And you?"

"The same." She took a nibble of the woodcock. "The

earl seems very pleased with you this evening," she said, having observed the distinction given to his great-nephew.

"So he does. He also seems very satisfied with Rawlinson. It's a good thing he came for a visit." Adam appeared to pick his words with care. "Rawlinson needs to learn more of his inheritance, the requirements of not only this estate but the several others he will get in due course. Mr. Chambers told me that the earl owns a number of holdings. Most are entailed, and one or two might be sold off if Rawlinson so chooses. But it is not good for a heir to be unacquainted with his property."

"It is odd, but I hadn't realized the earl owned so many places. I don't know why I should be surprised. 'Tis not uncommon." She gave Rawlinson a speculative survey.

"I just hope that Rawlinson appreciates what he receives."

The footman removed their plates and Emma subsided into silence. How could one tell if someone truly appreciated what he inherited? Caring for it, she supposed. Her father had been an astute manager of their property. What a pity he was not as clever when it came to his only child.

The cloth was removed and dessert brought in, and potted crawfish, preserved melon, white currants, and sliced peaches were placed close to where Emma and Adam sat. She saw Claude take a huge helping of the charlotte russe before him. He would get fat if he continued to stuff himself as he had this evening.

"I understand that Claude still insists you will marry him. How do you plan to escape that fate?" Adam glanced at her cousin, then back to Emma.

She closed her eyes for a moment, then faced Adam. "Frankly, I do not know. If I must, I will run away. The countess has indicated she will help me but as to how, I do not know."

"If there is anything I might do . . ." Adam began, before taking a breath and allowing his words to fade away. What could he offer? He had nothing. The peaches were bitter in his mouth. No one had promised that life would be fair. He must remember that the earl was giving him a splendid opportunity to train under one of the finest stewards in this county. But he wanted more and he couldn't have it.

How could he in all conscience ask the lovely young woman at his side to marry him? She had a dowry of five thousand pounds! That was more money than he could hope to earn in a lifetime. Could he swallow his pride to ask her, only to have her father laugh at his temerity? It was not a pleasant thought. He could not demean her by begging her to flee to Scotland with him, however much that notion appealed to him.

Emma gave Adam a troubled glance. He had begun to offer his help, then stopped. Why? Was he to allow his foolish pride to stand in the way of happiness? Not only hers but his? With her dowry they surely could purchase a modest estate. And with skillful management, which she was sure he possessed by now, their investment would improve.

Unless her father withheld her dowry! She peered down to the far end of the table where she could see her father casually chatting with the countess about something. The countess appeared to show interest in the topic. It was odd how he could manage to get along well with others and yet be so obtuse when it came to his daughter.

It would be frightful to return to her home after this party was over. How could she bear having *that woman* direct her every hour, nag her about marrying Claude—

as Emma was certain she would do, day in and day out. There was something in the looks directed at Emma that foretold Viola's nature. True, it was understandable that she would wish Emma from the house. Emma was a constant reminder of a previous marriage. There was little doubt but that the magnificent portrait of her mother had been banished to the attics. It would be so nice if Emma could marry and spirit off that portrait. It was all she cared to take.

Mrs. Turner offered no solace. She had ever been in Claude's pocket. Papa had turned off Emma's personal maid, Nancy. It helped that the countess now employed the girl, but it meant that when Emma returned to Brook Hall she would be terrifyingly alone.

With a determined effort, she shut her mind to the unpleasant prospect of her future. When the countess signaled that it was time for the women to leave the dining room, Emma took heart in Adam's surreptitious touch on her hand. It was oddly comforting rather than flirtatious. She gave him a hesitant smile as she gathered her gloves from her lap and rose. It would not be good to let her partiality show. Her father might take it into his head to insist upon announcing an engagement to Claude this evening!

Once free of the dining room and the sneering looks from Claude and her father's cold eyes, Emma was drawn to the side of the countess as they strolled to the vast drawing room.

"Please do not worry so. Your father may think he holds the winning cards, but I believe my dearest Charles will be able to foil his plans." The countess looked enormously pleased about something.

"I do not see quite how that may be, ma'am," Emma replied dubiously before an elated Gussie swished up to her looking as though she had won the lottery.

The countess drifted away to chat with other guests after murmuring words of encouragement to Emma.

Emma put her hands together. "Well, Gussie, are you going to tell me or shall I die of curiosity?"

"Never that! You must know—Rawlinson has asked Papa for my hand and of course Papa agreed. We are to announce our betrothal this evening!" She beamed a smile of joy at Emma.

"Quite as the earl planned, no doubt. He may be old, but I sense in him a schemer of the first water." Emma shared a smile with her good friend. What a wonderful thing to happen for her.

Gussie laughed as intended. "I would that he scheme on your behalf, in that event."

"The countess assured me that all will be well," Emma replied, again dubious as to how it might be achieved.

"Let us hope she is correct."

Louise joined them. "Gussie, you look like the cat that has sole possession of the cream pot."

"Now," Emma inserted, "you will know more later. Look, isn't Amelia's gown the prettiest thing you have ever seen?"

Louisa nodded, accepting that whatever Gussie's secret might be she would learn all before the ball was over.

In the dining room, the earl briskly suggested the gentlemen join their ladies. Rawlinson led the way after a nod from the earl. Mr. Lawrence gave his neighbor a puzzled glance before following the others.

Adam was surprised to find the earl taking his arm to lead him away from the drawing room. Being a sensible man, he waited politely to find out what the earl had on his mind.

The earl led him to the library that was not far from

the ballroom. "I wish to inform you of my decision regarding your future." He paused long enough to set Adam's heart to beating rapidly. "I am very pleased with the progress you have shown in estate management. Chambers says you have a gift for administration. He's been a superb steward, so he ought to know."

Adam grinned. "Thank you, sir. I can truthfully say it has been all my pleasure. I have never been so content."

"I do feel there is a lack, however." The earl gave Adam an assessing stare, one that somewhat intimidated him as well.

Adam's grin faded and he wondered what the problem might be. Had he failed in some regard? What had he left undone?

"You have surpassed the hopes I nurtured and impressed Chambers to a considerable degree. However, we both feel you need a greater challenge."

Adam waited, holding his breath, wondering what was to come next.

"Therefore, I have decided to give you a neat little estate south of here so you may expand your knowledge, secure that your efforts will be to your own benefit. Rawlinson agrees with me. The estate is not entailed and I may do with it as I please, but I am glad he feels as I do on this matter. Lavington Court is a pretty place. But, it needs a master on the premises."

"I hardly know what to say! Thank you very much, sir!" Adam gulped, scarcely able to comprehend his good fortune.

"Well, it seems the least I can do for such a promising landlord who also happens to be my great-nephew." The earl grasped Adam's arm and began slowly walking with him to the ballroom. "There is one little matter, though."

Adam held his breath. What condition would be tacked on to this almost-too-good-to-be-true gift?

"You will need a wife, no doubt of it. Otherwise the house will not receive the proper attention. Sophia informs me the house would benefit from a woman's touch. Most do."

Adam caught sight of the twinkle in his great-uncle's eyes and relaxed. "Have you someone in mind, perchance?"

The earl gave him a sage smile. "Perhaps. It has been pointed out to me that Claude is still being promoted as the future husband for Emma. I shudder to think of any young woman under his thumb. Do you believe *you* might come to have a fondness for her, my boy?"

Unable to restrain his grin, Adam nodded. "I believe that would not be the slightest problem, sir. I have come to love her dearly."

"Then ask her."

With the earl's blessing ringing in his ears, Adam left his side to find Emma.

The gathering had moved from the drawing room to the ballroom. Those who had not been invited to the dinner now arrived to enjoy an evening of dancing. It would not be like Bath, where the upper assembly ceased promptly at eleven of the clock. Tonight they might easily dance until dawn if they wished.

There was a spirit of expectancy in the air, particularly when it was observed how Viscount Rawlinson hovered about Augusta Dunlop, a local favorite. That her father looked as pleased as punch hinted at good news from that quarter.

The earl sought out Mr. Lawrence early on, sweeping that gentleman along with him to the terrace, where the two proceeded to talk in a manner far too businesslike to be suitable to a ball. Whatever was going on?

The gossiping ladies put their heads together to conjecture a feasible reason. It was impossible that a group consisting of a mere fifty couples could not miss the presence of so imposing a gentleman as the earl even for a short time.

When at last the two returned, the earl wore an enigmatic expression. Mr. Lawrence looked as though his dinner had not agreed with him.

Emma was far too busy to pay much heed to her father. Indeed, this was one evening when she wished she might forget he was around to plague her! Not to forget the charming Viola. She stood by Claude, anxiously peering at the terrace from time to time. Emma had to smile at the pair. Viola looked rather concerned, and Claude? Claude was far too wrapped up in himself to be aware that there might be trouble on the horizon.

Her oyster-white satin ball gown with lace decorating the very low neckline boasted her late mother's diamond pin centered at the front. The countess had insisted she carry a ravishing blue silk-gauze scarf that proved to be a nuisance. However, the effect of the unusual shade of blue against the oyster white was so fetching Emma decided to bear with it. Plus, she hadn't missed the warm expression in Adam's eyes when they exchanged looks. He appeared to approve.

Claude managed to sidle up to her when she returned to the countess following a lively Scotch reel. He extended his hand.

Emma gave him a puzzled look. Surely he didn't think she would willingly dance with him.

"After that unseemly activity, I should think you would be parched. Come with me and I shall see to it that you get some punch." He put his hand under her arm, forcibly ushering her to the side room, where a table was laden with punch and other beverages. Supper was to be after midnight.

"I truly do not wish for your company, cousin!" she declared in a quiet voice that, while firm, would not carry to embarrass the countess.

"But you must remember that your father has given his blessing to our marriage."

"Has he, now? You know, you are becoming so tiresome about this. I shall inform you one last time. I will never marry you, you clod." She took a sip of her punch and set the glass on a table before leaving the room—and Claude—behind.

She knew well that she had been improper in her refusal. It appeared useless to be polite to Claude. He had the thickest skull imaginable.

She had reckoned without his persistence. He came up behind her, took her arm, and without so much as a word, led her to where a set was forming for the next dance.

Emma seethed at his effrontery. Yet, she was not so lost to convention that she would walk away from him in full view of the assembled guests. Claude was one of those dancers who attempt to excel and end up overdoing. A quadrille had been called, and Emma had to wonder if he had something to do with that. Usually a lady would request a particular dance. When Emma caught sight of a smug Viola, she had her answer.

Claude was not content to jump lightly, he had to leap high enough to enable him to cross his legs several times before he came down. Emma was so embarrassed she wished she could slink away from him, but of course that would not do. When it came time to do the Hands Across, Claude dragged her along whether she wished it or not. She could not keep her disgust from showing in her expression. It was an unseemly display.

He may have thought he was showing off his skill, but he merely made himself look unrefined and boorish.

As soon as the last note was heard, she properly curtsied, then whisked away from the menacing Claude. At least her new white satin slippers had survived intact. That was the best she might say to his dancing ability!

"At last, I am able to reach your side. I vow that every gentleman here wishes to partner you," Adam teased when he placed her hand on his arm. "Do you wish to dance? Or would you prefer a stroll on the terrace?"

Emma darted a curious look at him. She had earlier caught a glimpse of the earl in conversation with her father. Had something been decided? Of course those gentlemen would not have bothered to inform her of anything. But . . . was it possible that her father had approved Adam? Would her father willingly relinquish his aim of having Claude marry his daughter? She doubted that. More likely she would be told what to do, and that would be the end of her future!

"The terrace, if you please. It is uncommonly warm for late July, is it not?" She matched her steps with his, unwilling to study his expression and so know what was on his mind. He could be bidding her farewell. He might go and she would never see him again. The very idea of such a thing made her ill.

The tall doors to the terrace had been left open. Between the heat of hundreds of candles and the exertions of the dancers, the cooler air was welcome. Light streamed forth from the many windows, creating bright stripes on the stone.

Emma glanced again at Adam, then down at the stone paving beneath her feet.

"Claude outdid himself in that last dance. Very athletic, your Claude."

There was a smile in Adam's voice that took any sting from the words, yet Emma took umbrage. "He will never be *my* Claude."

"Thank goodness for that!" They walked on for a time, then Adam spoke again after turning to face her. "I have some news for you."

Emma's heart sank to her satin slippers.

"My great-uncle has seen fit to bestow a fine—although modest, he tells me—estate on me. Rawlinson saw it once and says it is a capital piece of property. It has a fine house on it as well."

"You will need an experienced housekeeper, I think," Emma said with hope, her heart rising to nearly choke her.

"Indeed, the earl suggested that I look about for someone. In fact, he suggested I marry."

Emma gazed up to Adam's face, wishing the light were not so dim so she could gauge his feelings better. "Did he perchance suggest anyone in particular?"

"He did. I wonder that I dare to ask the young lady I desire to wed to marry with me. There is a gap between us."

"Is it money?" Emma queried, wondering at her boldness.

"It is. While I have the estate, it will take time to enlarge it to the point where I feel comfortable enough to seek her hand." He took both her hands in his, staring down at her with what she deemed a tender expression.

"Adam Herbert, I love you dearly. Will you ask me to marry you, for I vow I will have no other man as husband."

His crack of laughter was kind and he drew her close to him in careful regard. "There is nothing in this world that I wish more than to have you as my wife. The earl had a talk with your father earlier, and wrung permission from him, although I have not the least notion how. If you so please, we may have the banns called soon."

"This Sunday, dearest Adam. I long to begin a life with you at my side, to have our family."

"I'll write my father, for we'll wish him to perform the ceremony," Adam murmured before he lost himself in Emma's charms. Their kiss was all that he had hoped, and his dearest Emma proved she was not averse to a second and third. All of a sudden, life looked rather wonderful.

From the doorway the countess smiled in satisfaction.